to:

from:

ALSO BY T.D. JAKES

The
Memory
Quilt

A CHRISTMAS STORY
FOR OUR TIMES

T.D. JAKES

ATRIA BOOKS

New York   London   Toronto   Sydney

ATRIA BOOKS

A Division of Simon & Schuster, Inc.
1230 Avenue of the Americas
New York, NY 10020

First Atria Books hardcover edition November 2009

ATRIA BOOKS and colophon are trademarks of Simon & Schuster, Inc.

For information about special discounts for bulk purchases, please contact Simon & Schuster Special Sales at 1-866-506-1949 or business@simonandschuster.com.

The Simon & Schuster Speakers Bureau can bring authors to your live event. For more information or to book an event contact the Simon & Schuster Speakers Bureau at 1-866-248-3049 or visit our website at www.simonspeakers.com.

Designed by Stephanie D. Walker

Manufactured in the United States of America

10   9   8   7   6   5   4   3   2   1

Library of Congress Control Number: 2009034941

ISBN 978-1-4391-7045-8
ISBN 978-1-4391-7047-2 (ebook)

I would like to dedicate this book

To my beautiful wife, Serita, whose love
of the holidays always made me
seek deeper meaning to it all;

To my children whose bright eyes at Christmastime
were always my greatest gift from them;

To my sister Jacqueline whose birthday on Christmas
always made it extra special;

And to my older brother Ernest
who will always be my hero.

The Memory Quilt

$\mathcal{S}$he's filed," Jean said.

"What was that, dear?" Lela Edwards asked, hastily twisting the volume control knob on the clock radio, abruptly quieting "O Come, All Ye Faithful" to an unrecognizable muffle.

"'She's *filed*,' I said."

Phone conversations with Jean were like this—begun without much small talk. Barely a hello, and she was off with the subject like a sprinter at the sound of the gun.

"Darcie filed for divorce," she said, skipping a few beats before she added, "Mother, don't start."

"What am I starting? I'm just trying to understand what you're saying," Lela said.

Jean sighed. "Darcie filed for divorce yesterday." She said the words slowly, as if reluctant to repeat herself.

"I *thought* you said a few months ago that they were *thinking* of getting a divorce. Here the child's barely been married a year. Didn't they even *try* to work things out?"

"Mother, I'm just telling you what's going on."

Lela brushed away a speck of lint from her blue jersey knit skirt and glanced at the large clock on the wall next to the refrigerator in the long kitchen/dining area. Nine forty-five. She was supposed to leave in five minutes for the Wednesday women's Bible study and here she was hearing news like this. Barbara would be outside honking her horn soon, and nobody wanted to hear that "La Cucaracha" song that Barbara's son had installed in the car. At least she already had her coat on.

Jean made a noise, as if aware that Lela's attention had strayed. "She's coming here to Missouri City for Christmas, Mother, instead of what you and she talked about."

"She can't pick up a phone and tell her grandmama that?"

This was supposed to be the perfect Christmas—or near perfect. And that meant having all three of her daughters and her—she had to say—favorite granddaughter home for the holidays.

"Mother, you lecture."

"Lecture?"

"That's why *I'm* telling you. Besides . . . I want Darcie here with me, Mother. She's two months from her due date. This is the last time she can fly here."

"She lives in Indiana, Jean. She'd rather fly a thousand miles to Texas than drive here to spend Christmas with her grandmama like she promised?"

"Mother . . . she's feeling vulnerable right now—"

"And that's *another* reason why the girl don't need to be divorced." She tried to ignore the echo of her own lectures given to the girls over the years, filled with "Don't say *don't* if you mean *doesn't*."

"Now she's gonna be a single mother—" Lela thought out loud.

"Tell that to Doug, Mother. He's the reason this divorce is happening right now."

"I still don't understand—"

She was interrupted by the sound of a horn blaring the first notes of "Jingle Bells." Lela shook her head, grateful at least that the song had been changed to something less tacky than "La Cucaracha." "That's Barbara. I gotta go. We'll discuss this later."

"Mother . . ."

In the silence that followed, Lela suddenly sensed an ocean's worth of words left unsaid or words she wished had been unsaid over the years, washed along by a tide of unmet expectations. She was tired of swimming against the current. "I told you Barbara's waiting."

"Have you given any thought to what I suggested last week? About your moving here? The neighborhood's getting bad and—"

"Barbara's waiting, Jean."

"Okay. Love you." Yet Jean's words sounded a little reluctant.

"Love you too." Lela snapped off the radio, rubbing her shoulder as she stood. "Arthur" was kicking up today. She hoped her arthritis-strength ibuprofen was in her purse.

As she headed to the front door, she absently searched for Smokey—a stray she'd picked up around her garbage can the previous month. Somebody's throwaway, she surmised. The kitten had a weird grayish coloring that she could almost swear was blue (but cats weren't *blue,* were they?). She didn't know what kind of cat he was. But she'd named him after

Smokey Robinson, the famous R & B singer. She'd felt sorry for him until she got the bill to deworm him.

Barbara's horn sounded "Jingle Bells" again.

"Hold your horses," she said softly. Barbara couldn't hear her from this distance. She squeezed into her black pumps, knowing she would regret the choice later, before grabbing the purse and Bible waiting on an end table.

Wonder if I need a hat. She fingered the gray locks curling just above her shoulders. She stuck a hand out the door to get a sense of the temperature. Good. The weather was mild. She hated covering up her new haircut.

The wind picked up under a sky that was a weak pastel blue but didn't look to deposit snow anytime soon. The 45 degree temperature was too high for that. If the weather continued like this, it looked to be a brown Christmas in two weeks. That was fine with her. She hated driving in the snow.

Her best friend, Barbara Wiggins, at seventy-three—two years older—still liked to drive in any kind of weather, and so be it. Lela grunted as she folded herself into Barbara's silver PT Cruiser. The scent of bayberry—one of Barbara's favorite scents—immediately enfolded her.

"'Bout time," said Barbara, running a hand along her short, salt-and-pepper, mostly salt afro.

"Sorry. That was Jean on the phone. Told the girl I had to go."

"Jean? Everything okay?" Barbara put the car in gear. "O Holy Night" blared from WMBI on the radio.

Lela sighed, wondering how much to reveal. She didn't feel like getting into it with Barbara. "Everything's fine."

Barbara's glance was wry. "If you say so. As if I didn't know better judging by how you look right now."

"Just drive, girl."

"Yes'm." Barbara saluted, as she headed north—the only way they could go, with Laflin being a one-way street— toward Morgan Park.

Lela sighed as they passed the last of the bungalows on the long block of 117th and Laflin. This was the kind of residential neighborhood that some didn't believe still existed on the far southeast side of Chicago. People didn't expect more than projects, burned-out buildings, and crime stats here now. But there were still some houses around, even if they weren't looking as well kept up as they had been twenty years ago. Lela blamed the decline of the neighborhood

on the new blood on the block, some of whom—like the woman in the last house on the northeast corner—were merely renting. Key people, owners who acted as neighborhood watch people and were house-proud, had moved away over the years. There were more and more signs of a gang's influence now, with graffiti scrawled across an abandoned building here and there on 119th Street or even across a garage door.

Still, she was pleased to see that many of the houses at least were decorated for Christmas. More than a few houses boasted the large snow globe that the block club picked out. Surprisingly, the "newbies" knew how to follow instructions and kept things uniform.

Lela was one of the few residents left who had purchased the houses when they were built between 1963 and 1965. Her particular house was bought in 1964, a year after Barbara and her husband bought theirs. Walt and Lela were able to purchase the house only because the financing fell through for another couple bidding on it, an event she attributed to God's mercy.

The neighborhood hadn't changed much, ethnically speaking. It was still African American for the most part,

suggesting that racial segregation was still an issue in some parts of Chi-Town.

In less than fifteen minutes Barbara pulled up at the corner of 112th and Vincennes adjacent to the old Catholic school housing Briarwood Baptist. What a relief. Unlike on Sunday mornings, they didn't have to park two blocks away.

Lela's feet were already hurting from the tight shoes by the time they reached the red-brick fellowship hall, the first building north of the sanctuary. And they still had to descend a flight of stairs to the basement level and Fellowship Room 1, where the senior women's Bible study met. She grunted down each one, wondering not for the first time why the *senior* women had to struggle down the stairs while the *junior* women met on the first floor. Why couldn't they drag *themselves* down here and switch with the senior women? Maybe she would talk to Pastor about that.

She sighed as she entered the table-lined double room with its cream-colored walls, enlivened by framed posters depicting various types of flowers.

There were about fifty in the group and forty who showed up regularly. Since the church had made a considerable effort to combat the segregation evident on the South Side, different

races were represented. About thirty women were there now, carrying on the traditional "Christmas clash," with half the group in a myriad of red and green Christmas sweaters and the other half favoring jewel-toned sweaters (in purple, yellow, and blue)—all looking like living Christmas ornaments.

Estelle, the new widow, had shown up. *But,* Lela wondered, *why?* She was only forty-five, hardly senior. Most of the other women were fifty-five at least. And she usually dressed like a hussy, just like today. Here it was ten AM and she had on a skin-tight purple two-piece outfit like she was going to a club or something. She was slim and petite but now reminded Lela of a grape. *Who is she trying to impress?* Lela thought to herself.

Lela nodded a greeting. Her smile was much warmer as she turned to Nita Juarez, who promptly handed her a small, foil-covered bowl.

"Mole as promised," Nita said, a mischievous grin highlighting her impish face. "Put that over your chicken, okay?"

Lela smiled. "Girl, I might have gas as a result, but I'm sure gonna eat this. Thank you. Uh, *gracias.*"

Nita smiled and patted her arm as if Lela had performed a cute trick. "*De nada.*"

"Everybody get settled so we can get started, ladies." As usual, Lorraine Collins, the Bible study leader, didn't need a microphone. Her deep voice carried across the long fellowship room—a carryover from her work on the stock exchange several years back. She was tall—over six feet—and had an enviously flawless, chocolate brown complexion as well as a ramrod posture that the Army would have been proud of. She was also seventy but didn't look it.

"Last call for the coffee and doughnuts," added Donna Evans, the fifty-five-year-old, foot-shorter, auburn-haired (well, more and more silver streaks were starting to show) co-leader of the study. She wore a sweater with a snowflake pattern the main color of which matched her startling gray-blue eyes and highlighted her fair complexion.

Perhaps Donna shouldn't have mentioned the coffee and doughnuts, Lela surmised. Half the women already seated instantly gravitated toward the table. Another fifteen minutes passed before all were settled again.

"With this being the Christmas season, we have a challenge for you ladies," Lorraine announced. "For the next couple of weeks until Christmas, we'll follow the story of a woman who was very important to this season—Mary."

Lela's eyes opened wide. They hardly *ever* focused on Mary.

Donna held up several pink sheets. "I have a handout with nine Scripture passages. You can use it or read the passages in your Bible."

Estelle volunteered to pass out the handout, a move Lela saw as a sad bid for attention.

She shook her head, as she turned her attention to the passages listed on the sheet. Well, this was good for about a couple of days' reading. She couldn't see stretching this out for two weeks.

"We might think we already know all about Mary, but God has something fresh to teach us through her journey," said Lorraine. "When the Gospel of Luke first mentions her, Mary was probably just a young teen—someone you wouldn't pay much attention to. But we're going to pay some attention and in the coming weeks ask the Holy Spirit to open our hearts to what we can learn from the woman God considered highly favored."

Lela returned home at twelve thirty to a ringing phone and a loudly meowing kitten who greeted her at the door

demanding food. She answered the less insistent one first.

"I called your cell a hundred times," said Eileen, as soon as Lela picked up. Eileen lived in the house next door on the right with her eighty-two-year-old father, James. "Why didn't you pick up?"

Lela crunched down her irritation. "I don't like using it."

"Why have a cell phone if you don't use it?"

"I'm sure you called for a reason, Eileen." *And what is she doing home at this time of day? Why isn't she at work?* Lela thought.

"Daddy thinks he heard someone trying to break into your garage while you were away."

Lela listened but thought, *his imagination, more than likely.* Wasn't it only last month that he thought he heard someone breaking into her house and called the police? Turned out to be only the wind.

"When I passed your garage, your door was wide open," Eileen said.

Well, that got Lela's attention. But who, she asked herself, would break into a garage in the middle of the day? That took

some nerve. Maybe they had waited until she had left for church. Or it could have happened last night. That sounded more likely. She hadn't been out to her garage today. Was it the same person who broke into Barbara's garage a month ago?

The usual suspect was the kid across the street, who lived with his mother and her latest boyfriend. The little hooligan ran wild around the neighborhood and was probably in a gang by now. Lela shook her head. How was it that at thirteen, he had attitude to spare?

"Thanks for letting me know, Eileen."

"I'm making some fruitcake. You wanna come over for a slice?"

The last thing she wanted to do was go over to Eileen's. She didn't like Eileen's father, James, who had moved in after he suffered a heart attack. Eileen had made a feeble and embarrassing matchmaking attempt with Lela and the father the previous year.

Lela shook her head at that memory. She couldn't imagine why her neighbor would assume she'd be interested in an eighty-two-year-old man who continually grumbled at life, hardly bathed, and seemed a trifle senile. There was, after all,

that time when he mooned a couple of teens hanging out on the sidewalk in front of the house. The police were called on him that time, not the kids. Why Eileen thought Lela could handle a man like James was anybody's guess.

"Maybe some other time. Thanks, Eileen."

Better check that garage.

She switched shoes first, then braved the wind that now seemed decidedly frigid.

The heavy yellow door on the alley side of her detached garage was open at the bottom, but less than an eighth of the way. So much for it being wide open. It had to be a kid trying to match his thieving skills against her garage door. He lost, fortunately. She sighed, wondering if she needed to march across the street and confront Deborah about her son, Ronnie. Sometimes she caught him in the alley at night on his skateboard with a sly expression on his face. Maybe it wasn't the son at all, but the no-good boyfriend. What was his name again? Leo. He had to be no good if he couldn't marry her like any decent man and instead preferred to shack up. He was probably on drugs.

As she returned to the house, she felt restless and needing

of a task to complete. She had housework to do, of course, but she didn't feel like doing that just yet.

She drifted into her bedroom at the back of the house and peered into the large, red tote bag beside her bed, full of fabric she had had every intention to use to make Darcie and Doug a quilt with a double wedding ring pattern. She usually gave quilts to celebrate family weddings. But what with her mother dying last year, she hadn't gotten around to starting the quilt for this couple.

There was no need for it now, but she hated seeing good fabric going to waste.

She wandered aimlessly down the hall to the living room and switched on the lighting even though the drapes were wide open. Two years ago, her daughters had banded together to get the living room redone with track lights highlighting an Annie Lee print on the wall adjacent to the closet. It featured a church scene and a mother forcing a child to give up her gum. She had arranged the print above the black Ikea sideboard upon which the latest photos of her daughters sat.

Tamara, her oldest, was on the left, with Jean in the middle and the youngest, Sylvie, on the right. All had her ochre

complexion, highlighted by her husband Walter's sassy smile. Only Jean still kept her hair long.

Jean had given her the Annie Lee print, laughingly saying that it reminded her of their relationship.

Smokey suddenly made his presence in the living room known by bellowing his feed-me-now song.

"I'm not thinking about you right now." It wasn't quite time for him to be fed anyway. She perched on the green and white floral print couch and pulled a photo album out of the coffee table drawer.

As she opened it, touching the carefully decorated plastic-covered pages (Sylvie's handiwork), the always present ache of missing Walt increased. The stubborn old man would have to have a fatal heart attack in February, the same year Mama died—2008. That was certainly a year she wanted to forget. This year, they would've been married fifty years.

She flipped through the photos, pausing at one of her favorites. Every year they took a photo of the girls sitting on the couch in the same birth order spots. In this one, Tamara was thirteen and wearing a big afro. Jean, eleven, with her customary ponytail and long bangs, frowned in the middle, while seven-year-old, pigtailed Sylvie, on the right, smiled.

It was only later that she realized why Jean frowned. Tamara had been picking on her. Lela shook her head. Tamara had been good at stealth picking—the whispered comment just when she thought her mama's back was turned.

An hour passed before she looked up from the photo album with the sudden realization that she had a task: begin the reading for Bible class.

She thought of putting a load of clothes in the washing machine first . . . and then the phone rang. She answered and found Barbara on the other end.

"Got a favor to ask. I'm on the angel tree committee—"

"You're on *every* committee at church, Barbara Wiggins."

"If I might finish, Lela Edwards." She was amused by the little jab. "We were wondering if you wouldn't mind making a small quilt for the ministry."

"You know I only do quilts for the family."

"I know, but—"

"And I'm not sure I can have one done by Christmas anyway, even though I have all that fabric I never used for Darcie's quilt." She sighed heavily. "I wish I *had* gotten to it. Guess it's too late now . . ."

Barbara was silent for several moments before saying,

"Okay, what happened? I knew something was wrong the moment you got in the car."

No use beating around the bush. "It's Darcie. She's filed for divorce."

"Does that surprise you? They've been having problems all year from what you told me."

"They've only been *married* a little over a year. They could've worked those out."

"Didn't he *cheat* on her? Twice?"

"Do we have to talk about this?"

"Fine. So, are you gonna make a quilt? I felt a nudge by God that maybe you should make a quilt for us."

Lela suddenly felt manipulated by the mention of God. "Why would I give Darcie a wedding ring quilt *now*?" She thought out loud. Everyone else she'd given a quilt to was still married. Had she failed Darcie and jinxed the marriage by *not* giving her the quilt?

"I'm not talking about Darcie. Make a quilt for the angel tree ministry. There are a number of needy children—"

"I don't make quilts for children. Besides, all they want are those fancy comforters these days. They don't know how to appreciate a quilt."

"Does that have anything to do with your making it or not?"

"You should stop being so pushy, old woman."

"That's what friends are for, Le."

"I'll think about it. Talk to you later about this."

She hung up and returned to the bedroom to gather dirty clothes to wash. As she did though, her attention turned to the red tote bag of fabric. Smokey was perched on it.

"Cat, get off that fabric!"

But Smokey paid her no heed.

It was just as well. Making a quilt was the last thing she wanted to do right now.

2

*T*he steady *thump-thump-thump-thump, ba-dump* of music forced its way through the walls into her consciousness, driving her to wakefulness.

"What on earth?"

To add insult to injury, her right shoulder throbbed, as if in time to the music. She slowly sat up, gazing about the dark room. A small, dark lump slid down the pillow next to hers. She soon felt Smokey's soft fur brush against her elbow. Why wasn't he in *his* bed? She didn't like him shedding fur or possibly peeing on her new blue, green, and white comforter or on her new flannel sheets.

Once more the thump of music assaulted her ears. *What time is it?*

She fumbled for her glasses and the lamp on the bedside

table. *Two AM. Where on earth is that noise coming from?* Grumbling, she threw back the covers. First things first. She grabbed Smokey and plunked him in the small doggy bed by the dresser, then padded into the living room. A peep through the curtains showed lights on in the last house across the street and cars littering the curb at that end.

Deborah and her boyfriend throwing a party, probably. *I should've known.* The phrase "Everything is copasetic"—a phrase people used in the sixties—inexplicably came to her mind. But everything was definitely *not* satisfactory. Her hands clenched, rage building within her.

She seemed to have only one emotion lately in regard to the members of that household: anger. The idea of them blasting music while decent folks were trying to sleep! *Lord, you know I need my sleep!* She had half a mind to call the police and half a mind to march across the street and give them a piece of her mind.

But in the middle of her internal debate, a police cruiser made its way along the street. Someone evidently had saved her the trouble. But instead of feeling relieved, she still felt enraged.

Now her head throbbed, and that usually led to nausea

if she didn't head it off at the pass. *Lord, don't let me have a stroke here.* Her hands shook as she poured herself a glass of water and quickly downed two ibuprofen. The music soon died down and she prayed to get back to sleep quickly.

Her prayer was answered. The next thing she knew, the cat's plaintive meow had awakened her and the hour was 6:00 AM Thursday. Her usual time of rising was difficult to face, thanks to the neighbors. But she was never one to laze around in bed.

Once more, there was Smokey sitting up on the end of her bed. "You little scamp. Got up here again, huh? Maybe I can train you to do something useful like get the newspaper for me."

She sat up, still feeling the slow burn of anger from earlier that morning. Her right shoulder throbbed again. Putting on her robe proved to be a challenge.

The morning also brought a snowfall under a slate blue sky that yesterday's temperature hadn't foreshadowed. Outside she saw a newspaper-shaped hole in the snow on her front walkway; someone had obviously stolen her *Sun-Times*. She exhaled.

After a quick shower, she couldn't ignore the call of the

open Bible on her dining room table, the book beckoning as she set about getting breakfast—putting on the teakettle and making oatmeal in the microwave.

Out of milk. Gotta go to the store. She could have kicked herself for not checking beforehand.

Just as she debated about what to do, the phone rang. "I'm running out to the store later today. Need anything?" Barbara's cheerful voice queried.

Thank you, Lord, she thought. "Milk, thanks, and—" She quickly inspected her refrigerator. "A dozen eggs. Forgot to get some when I was at the store last. 'Preciate it."

"I won't be back until noon though. Can you wait that long?"

Lela glanced at her now congealed bowl of oatmeal. "I guess so." The day stretched ahead of her. She had nothing but time.

After she boiled herself her last two eggs and had a slice of turkey bacon, there was no excuse. She had to start reading. In her large-print Bible, she turned to Luke 1.

Why don't you work while you listen to the Scriptures? The thought popped into her head with a suddenness that seemed to have God's prompting all over it. But there was nothing to work on. Still, she *could* listen to the Scriptures.

Now, where were those CDs? She fished around in the bookcase in the living room, almost knocking over Walt's picture. She stopped briefly to look at it, remembering the day that picture was taken—at the wedding of her niece Ruth, her oldest brother Oby's daughter. Walt looked handsome in his black suit and black and gold tie, a reminder of his old fraternity, Alpha Phi Alpha.

A ten-minute search soon produced the Bible on CD that Jean had insisted on giving her last Christmas. The Scriptures were read by a series of famous actors, pastors, and other celebrities, some of whom she'd never heard of. She hadn't listened to the CDs, preferring to use her well-worn Bible. But now she found herself opening the package or at least struggling to get through the plastic wrap and tape.

Finally, she set the CD with all the Gospels in the CD player and skipped ahead to the Gospel of Luke and the story of the announcement of Jesus' conception to his mother, Mary—Luke 1:26–38, the first Scripture passage on her Bible study list.

An actor's smooth baritone voice filled the room. She listened to the story all the way through, enjoying the dramatization, before starting the MP3 again.

"You have found favor with God." The angel's words caught hold in her mind, as if God was in the process of shaping something in her, something still formless like a gem that hadn't yet been cut and polished. She was also reminded that in a time when the Romans ran things and a woman was treated like a second-class—no, third-class—citizen, Mary must have felt anything *but* favored in Palestine.

She could relate. Like so many other African Americans, Walt and she had moved up to Chicago in 1962, hoping to find a Promised Land of more opportunities and equal treatment. They found not favor, but rather a pipe dream, at that point.

Her shoulder began to twinge, which sent her to look for the painkilling pills. As she poured herself a glass of water to wash the medicine down, the thought that she should be working on the quilt came to her and seemed to remain like a guest who wouldn't leave when asked. The question for her now was, *How am I supposed to sew if my shoulder's acting up?*

After half an hour, she started to feel a little better. Her thoughts swung from the Scripture to the quilt pieces. She headed to her room to at least look at the fabric. Once again,

Smokey was lying on top of the bag. She shooed him off and clucked over the cat hairs on the cream, tan, peacock blue, and cranberry fabrics—fabrics that went well with the color scheme of the condo Darcie and Doug had bought.

The fabrics—both old and new—brought back memories she hadn't really relished facing a year ago. But now, what type of quilt could she make, if not for Darcie's use? Who else in the family was getting married? Her brother Frank's daughter, Catherine? She had a fiancé she was bringing to Frank's on Sunday. Lela could make a quilt for them. But the thought didn't settle well with her, especially since she wasn't exactly sure when the youngsters were getting married.

She hauled the tote into the kitchen and set it by the table, along with a few magazines she'd recently bought that featured quilt patterns.

Humph. Seemed like all these magazines featured baby quilt patterns. She *never* made baby quilts. Quilts were far too precious to give to a baby, who would outgrow and not appreciate it anyway.

Yet one pattern in particular struck her immediately: a pieced quilt with nine colorful blocks. On each block was a

cheerful, baby-friendly item: a smiling sun, a heart, a toy box, a car, a ball, a baby's foot, a cat, a bird, and a bear—all for a baby to touch.

Could this be God trying to push her into making a quilt, like Barbara suggested? She shook her head. Surely *she* recognized the Holy Spirit's nudging in her own life. She firmly closed the magazine.

It was midafternoon when she heard a quick knock at the back door, followed swiftly by it opening. She'd left it unlocked for Barbara, who usually walked in without ringing the doorbell.

Barbara entered, stamping and brushing snow off her olive green wool coat. "Ooh, girl, the hawk is out today!" she announced as she plunked a gallon of skim milk and a plastic bag on the table.

Lela nodded at the aptness of the epithet. "Yep. It's definitely cold." She placed the jug in the refrigerator. "Got time to stay a bit? I'm putting the kettle on for tea. Are you hungry?"

Barbara shook her head. "My cholesterol's been high lately. I need to cut down on rich food, at least until Christmas. The kids are expecting a good meal that involves butter and

none of that Mrs. Dash stuff. Maybe I can lose a few pounds before then." Barbara patted her stomach.

Lela laughed. Barbara said the same thing every year—three or four times a year—and didn't seem to lose any weight. She still remained a size 18 and didn't seem all that bothered by the fact either, despite her words. She was seventy-three and looked like a woman twenty years younger. Besides, Lela mused, it wasn't as if *she* didn't have a hard time squeezing into size 12s herself.

"Sidney's coming, right?"

Barbara nodded, a satisfied smile on her face. "Bringing my grandbabies."

Lela thought Sidney's daughter and son—aged eight and twelve respectively—were little hellions, but she didn't feel the need to say so out loud. They were Barbara's grandkids, after all. She had the usual grandmother blind spot.

The phone suddenly rang. Jean began talking before she could get out a hello. "Mother, I need to talk to you about something."

"Can I call you back, Jean? Barbara's over and—"

"I just got a notice in the mail from the Social Security Administration. According to them, you're dead."

"What?"

"What's happening?" Barbara asked.

Lela clamped a hand over the wall phone's receiver. "Jean said the Social Security office is claiming I'm dead."

Barbara shook her head. "That's just what happened to that lady on whatchamacallit—*Datelines.*" Barbara sometimes placed a plural where it didn't belong.

"If they say you're dead, they'll stop your benefits," said Jean. "Maybe you should go by the office. What's the nearest one to you?"

"I need to check. Talk to you later."

"So, what are you going do?" Barbara asked, just as Lela hung up.

"Straighten this mess out, I hope. Know where the Social Security office is?"

"There's one off Eighty-seventh Street, I think. Good thing I came today." Barbara quickly grabbed her keys. "You ready?"

"Can I put on some boots at least?" Lela wiggled a socked foot.

At the Social Security office, the half hour Lela waited in line felt like an eternity. Ultimately, she was allowed to

approach a harassed-looking woman in a vastly unflattering walnut brown pullover sweater. At least it matched her skin perfectly.

"I've been told that I'm dead. How do I clear up this mess?" She tried to ignore the stares her remark generated.

"Uh, did you receive a letter or something?" asked the woman behind the counter.

"No, but my daughter said she did."

"Social Security number?"

Lela rattled it off, after thinking about it for a minute.

The woman typed the numbers into the computer, then spent another eternity looking at the screen. "Not again." She heaved a long sigh. "You're right. According to this, you've just been declared dead. Just a minute." She tapped away at the computer, while Lela tapped her boot against the scarred tile floor. "I need to see some ID."

Lela pulled out her driver's license, then waited impatiently while the woman crossed the room to talk to another woman, a dark-rooted blonde. The second woman at least had on a better choice of sweater—a red one in keeping with the holiday season. They both returned to the first woman's computer and stared at the screen as if it held life's greatest secrets.

"Will this affect my check?" asked Lela, to remind them of her presence.

"We'll have to look into this, ma'am," said the second woman. "Do you have a birth certificate or a copy of the letter you were sent?"

Lela stared at both women. "I haven't been *sent* a letter. I just said my daughter was. I don't understand why I have to prove that I'm still alive! Obviously I am."

"If you don't want your benefits canceled, you'll need to bring in proof that you're who you say you are. Do you have a birth certificate?"

"I don't carry it around with me!" She mentally went through the places at home where she might have put it. In the desk drawer in the kitchen?

"What time do you close today?"

The woman in brown glanced at her watch. "In three minutes."

Where has the day gone? She thought.

"We open at nine in the morning."

"But—" Lela began.

"When you return, you'll need to bring the letter your daughter received. Have a nice holiday season."

Grumbling, Lela followed Barbara to the car. Snow was falling in earnest now, as if to make up for lost time. At least *she* wasn't driving. Still, the crawl back to 117th was taking a lot longer than usual, even for Barbara.

"I should've gone local instead of taking the Ryan," Barbara said ruefully. "Going to club meeting tonight? Don't forget we're at Levon's."

The club—a widows' club—consisted of one of Lela's sorors from Delta Sigma Theta, one from Barbara's sorority—Zeta Phi Beta—and two women from church with whom they used to play bridge. They got together socially and even went on vacations together.

"Don't feel up to it tonight, not with the snow coming down like it is." She didn't feel up to the chatter of women tonight. The hole Walt left was too near the surface.

She opened her door to a ringing phone and a meowing cat. She answered the phone while she reached into the cabinet to take care of the cat. It was Jean again. "I've heard from you more times in two days than I normally hear from you in a month." As soon as Lela said the words, she regretted them.

"Would you rather I didn't call?"

"Jean, I—"

"I just called to see how it went at the Social Security office."

"I have to bring my birth certificate and prove that I'm still alive. And I need a copy of the letter they sent you."

"I can scan it and email it."

"You know I don't know how to retrieve attachments."

"Mother, I don't know why you don't. Doug showed you when he set up the computer."

"A computer that's not working that good anyway." Somehow there had to be a spiritual correlation between that computer and the end of Darcie and Doug's marriage.

"Do you need some help with the computer?"

"How can you help if you're almost a thousand miles away?"

"Mother, I just thought if you needed help, I can get somebody to—"

"Sylvie's not too far away. She's only at Indiana Wesleyan." Not that she saw Sylvie or her husband much these days. His name was Paul, but everyone called him Bean, since he often depicted beans in his artwork. And Bean was the name of his graphics art company.

"She's there until next Tuesday, when she goes to her

in-laws. You know this is her year for that, unless you were planning on her coming home this year." Jean's tone sounded a little bitter.

Why did everything have to turn into an argument with Jean? Lately, Lela seemed to get along better with Jean's husband, Chris. He was like Walter in so many ways—less emotional and more laid-back.

"I know Sylvie can't come home this Christmas, Jean. And Tamara's also going to her in-laws."

"I just called to check on you. What's the closest grocery store to you that accepts faxes? Jewel on 115th?"

"I don't usually shop at that one."

"Mother, just find a place for me to fax the letter and I'll send it there. Let me know by tomorrow, okay? Talk to you later." Jean hung up before Lela could get a word out.

Lela glanced at Smokey, who was currently rolling around the beige carpet in the dining area. She almost wished she had had cats instead of daughters.

*S*mokey's insistent and persistent meowing drove her out of bed that Friday morning an hour later than her usual time. As she slipped on the only slippers she could find—a pair with cheerful monkey heads, a gift from a grandchild years ago—she felt a not-so-usual nip in the air.

She usually turned the heat down at night, but the house felt practically Arctic. She suddenly felt like burying her face in Smokey's soft, warm fur. But there was not enough of him to make a good muff.

She glanced at the thermostat, which read 55 degrees. She tried to make the adjustment but didn't hear the heat come on. "Lord, you know I don't need to be up here in a cold house, now," she whispered.

She dialed her brother's number, hoping he'd excuse the early call.

Her sister-in-law Rhoda answered the phone as usual. Even after their fifteen years of marriage, she still felt more comfortable talking to her brother than to her sister-in-law. In fact, she usually felt more comfortable talking to Frank than to any of her other four brothers. "Frank there?"

"Oh, hey, Lela. He's at his men's Bible study. They meet at the crack of dawn. Want me to tell him you called?"

Lela bristled at what seemed to be Rhoda's not-so-subtle attempt to get off the phone. "I need someone to take a look at my furnace. Tell him to call me when he gets back, hear?"

"He won't get back until ten. I think he was going to call you about something anyway today."

Lela hung up, annoyed at Frank's absence and hoping that what he wanted to talk about didn't involve another family problem. She didn't have time for another thing right now. She took a longer shower than normal, trying to warm up before putting on a pair of jeans and a red wool sweater. When that was done, she plugged in a space heater to get some warmth in the house and decided to make tea.

Just as she put the tea kettle on, the phone rang. "What you up to today?" asked Barbara.

"I need someone to look at my furnace, ASAP. I don't think it's working properly."

"Want me to call Eddie? You remember Stefan's grandson from the Fourth of July barbecue I had? He works on furnaces."

Lela forced herself not to snort at the mention of Barbara's boyfriend—the usually effervescent Stefan, who always reminded her of a slick used-car salesman. He once talked her ear off for a whole hour. A boyfriend at her age, and a man ten years younger than her too. Lela remembered the relationship and her disapproval of it.

"Eddie available today?"

"I can call him and find out."

Lela grunted. Maybe God *was* looking out for her.

The call was soon made, and by ten, Eddie had pulled up in a van bearing the logo of the heating and cooling company. Lela remembered from Barbara's party the stocky young man with large, sleepy-looking eyes and an expression of permanent boredom. She also remembered his having a

toothpick in his mouth then as he had now. Bad habit, she guessed, unless he was trying to quit smoking. She thought she remembered Barbara saying something to that effect.

Barbara, looking pleased, bridged the seven-house gap between their houses just as Eddie arrived.

"Mrs. Edwards," Eddie greeted Lela in a voice that was moderately alert and friendly. "Barbara said your furnace wasn't working."

"It certainly isn't! You'll see that for yourself the moment you walk in."

As she led the way down the basement stairs, Lela couldn't help recalling all of the work Walt had done on the basement, especially for the girls, who used to hang out with their friends down there. The seventies-era walnut paneling, which the girls always said was old-fashioned, was still there.

Eddie grunted as he poked around in the furnace, flashlight in hand.

"What do you think is the problem?"

"Hmm," he replied.

"Hmm? What does that mean?" *He can hmm on his own time and on his own dime.* If she was to pay him, she needed more than that, she thought.

But Eddie just said "hmm" again. It was ironic that Stefan, a man who had once talked at her for thirty straight minutes about the best place in Chicago for ribs, had a grandson of so few words.

"Let's let the man work and get out of his hair."

Lela finally allowed Barbara to lead her back upstairs.

"He doesn't like people looking over his shoulder," Barbara explained. "He's really good at what he does, if you're worried."

"I ain't worried." But she was.

The image of the bag of fabric briefly came to her mind. She glanced at it still sitting beside the table. *How am I supposed to work on a quilt in this cold house?* She returned it to its rightful place in her bedroom.

Eddie ventured upstairs after an hour, just as Lela had brewed a second cup of tea and brought out the Pepperidge Farm Chessmen cookies. "When's the last time you had a furnace inspection?" He helped himself to a cookie, to Lela's annoyance.

"I meant to have it done well over a year ago . . . when Mama got sick," Lela said to Barbara.

"I remember."

"Well, I don't have good news, then. You need a new blower."

"How much is that gonna cost?"

"I'm estimating between three fifty and five hundred dollars. That's the best I can do. Sorry."

Lela exhaled loudly. "Can I do without it?"

"Not if you want heat. I wouldn't advise your putting it off in the middle of winter. Supposed to snow more today."

"Well, I guess that means I can't spend a lot of money on the grandkids this year. Hadn't counted on getting the furnace fixed."

"I'm sure they'll understand," said Barbara. "That's why I called earlier—to see if you wanted to do some Christmas shopping."

Lela threw a pointed look at Eddie.

"I can get the part, but can't get back here to install it until tomorrow. Got another job I need to take care of."

Lela sighed, suddenly realizing she hadn't prayed at all—not about the furnace and certainly not about the quilt. She breathed a quick "Give me wisdom, Lord," before turning back to Eddie. "Go ahead and get the part, then." She knew

she sounded ungracious but couldn't help herself. "And what time would you be back?"

"Around ten."

"You can't get here any earlier?"

Eddie merely shrugged, then helped himself to another cookie.

Guess that means no. "I'll see you at ten sharp then, hear?" She turned to Barbara. "Let's go. I'm tired of sitting here in a cold house."

"Let's get to Target. I'll be glad to drive. And you can spend the night at my house. You shouldn't stay in a cold house. Just give me fifteen minutes and I'll come back with the car. We can move Smokey down first, get him situated. I'll keep Al's dog in the den. She won't bother Smokey." Barbara's daughter, Alicia, kept a spoiled absolutely rotten Pekingese named Libby.

"This is all a nuisance!" Lela said, her gaze fixed on Eddie as if the whole thing were his fault.

He shrugged again, seemingly undisturbed by either her remark or her look.

"Can we also stop at the Jewel?" Lela asked Barbara. "Jean

said she'd fax her letter there. Also, can we swing by Social Security before we go shopping? I need to take my birth certificate over there."

Barbara saluted as she followed Eddie out the front door.

Coaxing Smokey into the cat carrier was a job that ate up almost an hour, what with him hiding under the table and then under the couch, before he could be pulled out and stuffed unceremoniously into the carrier and loaded into Barbara's car.

They had to endure his yowls on the short trip to Barbara's bayberry-scented house, and then the frustrated yips of Libby. Smokey was dumped in Barbara's spare room, along with his travel litter box. Since she would have to use that spare room, Lela wasn't exactly in favor of having the litter box there but would put up with it for now.

As they headed back out to the street, where Barbara's car was still running, Lela suddenly noted the whistle of a toy train running the perimeter of a village on a card table.

"Whoops! Thought I switched that off. Alicia insists on it every year," said Barbara.

Lela shook her head at the notion of a forty-year-old

woman insisting on having a train or anything else on in her mama's house.

She was glad Barbara volunteered to drive. Thick snow-flakes had begun to fall, like on a picture postcard, but the streets were somewhat treacherous with the salt trucks still on standby. At least they didn't have to go any farther than Eighty-seventh Street.

After picking up Jean's fax, Barbara took the Dan Ryan at an unusually slow pace, which ensured that they would arrive at the office a good forty minutes later, Lela guessed. She was almost exactly right.

The line was shorter at the Social Security office than it had been on the previous day. After showing her birth certificate and the letter Jean faxed, Lela signed a document to show her handwriting. She was feeling almost cheerful at being assured that the problem would be cleared up in no time.

She stopped herself, though, from saying aloud, "Make sure it is, hear?" to the man behind the counter. Instead, she returned to the car, where Barbara was listening to Christmas music on WMBI.

"All set?" she asked.

"We'll see."

"Target?"

"It's your car."

The drive to Target on 118th was even longer, thanks to the increase in snowfall, and the breakfast she had eaten earlier had long since worn off. Lela's stomach began to growl the moment Barbara pulled up in the parking lot.

"Might as well get a sandwich at the cafeteria here," Barbara suggested.

At Lela's insistence, they entered through the door closest to the small cafeteria. As they did, she was met with an unpleasant surprise: Deborah, the young woman in the corner house across the street, was behind the counter. The last person she wanted to see.

"I didn't know she worked in the cafeteria here," Lela whispered.

"Oh, yeah, she's been working here at least six months. You must not come that often if you haven't seen her."

"I come often enough, Barbara Wiggins," Lela huffed.

As usual, Deborah had on enough makeup for two people. Yet there was something hangdog about her expression

today, as if she'd received a blow to her spirit that two coats of makeup couldn't hide.

As they approached the counter, Lela expected a look of defiance or rolled eyes—looks automatic to young people with attitudes, people who threw wild parties at two AM.

But a wan smile lit Deborah's pixieish, heart-shaped face. "What can I get for y'all?"

Somewhat taken aback by Deborah's friendliness, Lela ordered a pretzel and lemonade; suddenly she was not in the mood for anything else. She half listened to Barbara's conversation with Deborah and was relieved when they sat to eat.

"I've got a list of stuff to get for the angel tree. What do you need to get here?"

"Something for Darcie at least. I'll need to send it to Texas, I guess, since she's in Missouri City with her mama."

"If you can't find something here, we can go to Bath and Body Works in Chicago Ridge Mall. They have some inexpensive stuff. Let's meet up in about half an hour, okay?"

Lela shrugged and ventured over to the beauty aisle, then wandered down to the jewelry and purse sections. But she couldn't get the haunted face of Deborah out of her mind,

images aided by the glimpses of the young woman at the cafeteria whenever she passed that way. She was more than glad when they left for Bath and Body Works.

At least some of the salt trucks made the rounds to get the streets cleared for rush hour. Nevertheless, Lela was glad to see their neighborhood.

"Wanna drop off your stuff? That way you won't forget anything at my house."

"Might as well. I need to get a change of clothes if I'm to spend the night."

Just as they approached her end of Laflin, a sprinkling of teens and preteens rounded the corner from 117th. She recognized Ronnie, walking by himself—recognized him by his huge, wildly blowing afro, a throwback to the seventies, a decade even his mama had never seen. He had delicate, almost pretty features, like his mother.

"Is that a police car in front of your house?" Barbara asked, as she parked in the only free space in that vicinity—across the street from Lela's house and a few houses down from Deborah's.

"Looks like they're talking to Eileen. I thought she would be at work at this time of day." Two police officers—a

Caucasian and an African American—leaned against the railing on Eileen's porch, listening as she seemed to punctuate every statement with an energetic gesture. Lela had seen the latter officer around the neighborhood before, thanks to Eileen's father's frequent calls and some problems with vandalism. "I hope it has nothing to do with whoever's trying to break into our garages."

"Maybe James called them. He's always calling the police on somebody," Barbara said.

"Looks like the police are leaving."

"I'm gonna run over and talk to Eileen and find out what's going on."

"And I better check the garage right quick and see if anyone tried to break into *it*."

Lela was halfway to her garage when she had a sudden thought: had they left Barbara's car unlocked? She could not remember, but she hurried to check the garage. But the garage doors looked untampered with, to her relief. It occurred to her that she should take her purchase into the house, given that Barbara was in a blabbing mood.

When she returned to the street, the police car was gone and the doors to Barbara's car were indeed unlocked, to her

chagrin. As she collected her bags from the back seat of the car, she could have sworn a bag was missing. She searched under the front seat. Not there.

As she went to put her bags in the house, Lela scanned the street for any likely thieves. There was Barbara, waving to her from Eileen's porch. Eileen's father, James, had joined them there. Eileen favored her father in looks, both being light-skinned with the sharp features that indicated someone of a different race somewhere in their family tree. While Eileen's hair was still dark (or as dark as a dye bottle could make it, Lela mused), James's hair was a sparse gray. With his neatly trimmed mustache and high cheekbones, he retained a shadow of the handsome man he undoubtedly was when he was younger. He usually wore suspenders and a bow tie—a nod to a bygone era of dapper dressing. Today was no exception.

"I'm telling you, the police won't do nothing about it," James was saying as Lela walked up. "We gotta do something *ourselves* to stop this foolishness!"

"Daddy," Eileen warned.

"What happened?" asked Lela.

"Daddy called the police again."

"I'm telling you, I heard someone in the alley last night. And I was right, wasn't I? Wasn't I, huh?"

"Somebody broke into *our* garage this time." Eileen sighed heavily. "They took the lawn mower. Had to leave work early to deal with this mess."

"Didn't you notice it was missing when you got in your car?" Eileen was a little scatterbrained. It was sometimes hard to believe that she was a pharmacist.

"I didn't put the car in the garage last night. I parked on the street, although I wish I hadn't, with all this snow." Eileen leaned closer to Lela and Barbara. "Daddy was having one of his episodes last night." She glanced at her father.

Lela snorted. Episodes? Was that another way of saying she found him drunk again or found him mooning another teenager?

Barbara patted Eileen's hand. "Well, listen, Eileen, you take it easy."

As they returned to Barbara's car, Lela asked, "Did I leave a bag at the Bath and Body works? I can't find Darcie's bath oil anywhere."

"I saw you take it out of the store. Why? Is it missing?"

Lela nodded. "I forgot to lock the doors when I went to

check my garage. Someone could have grabbed it out of the car while both our backs were turned."

A second search failed to uncover the one bag from Bath and Body Works. Lela could have kicked herself for not taking Barbara's advice and throwing her bags in the trunk with hers.

"Oh, Le, I'm sorry. We were only in Eileen's house a minute or two. You didn't hear this part, but her father's convinced that Ronnie's been breaking into the garages around here. I don't think he has, though."

Ronnie. Hadn't she just spotted the boy earlier coming home from school or from wherever he happened to be? Maybe *he* stole her bag. She soon voiced the thought.

"We don't know that he did."

"But we don't know he *didn't* steal it. I have half a mind to call the police myself."

Barbara sighed. "But what if he *didn't* steal it? You don't have any proof that he did. Anybody could have taken it." She fumbled in her purse for her wallet. "Here. I'll give you the money to replace what was stolen."

"Why would you do that? He's the one who needs to replace that bath oil."

"I say give him the benefit of the doubt. Now can we quit arguing about this?"

Lela folded her arms. "I'm not taking your money, Barbara."

"Well, would you at least go in and get your stuff so we can get inside out the cold? You, uh, might want to bring your quilting stuff, hint, hint." She grinned.

"I haven't decided I'm making a quilt, and I don't *need* you bugging me about it, old lady." But as usual, Barbara had a way of lightening her mood.

She quickly gathered toiletries and a change of clothes and returned to Barbara's car, flashing a smug smile in response to Barbara's snort and roll of the eyes—*her* response to Lela's lack of quilting paraphernalia.

Barbara doesn't always know what's best—certainly not what's best for me, Lela thought.

*I*t is true: if you don't like the weather in Chicago, just wait a few hours and it will be sure to change. A few minutes before ten on Saturday, Lela trudged through the slush—thanks to a 46 degree temperature—to the house to wait for Eddie's arrival.

She could hear the phone ringing as soon as she walked through the side gate. Oh gracious. I forgot to let the girls know where I was. They might be worried. The ringing stopped the moment she unlocked the door.

But just as she dialed voicemail to listen to her messages, Eddie's van pulled up in front of the house. She hung up, just as the first message—Jean's—began.

"Morning, Mrs. Edwards." He still had a toothpick in his mouth. Whether it was the same one from the previous day, Lela could only guess.

She looked at her watch. *I guess ten minutes after ten is ten sharp, huh?*

But Eddie didn't seem to be fazed by the action. At least he went to work right away on the furnace.

So did she. Plugging in the space heater and putting the kettle on had now become a routine. She decided as well to listen to Scripture. Instead of the fancy CD player in the black Ikea sideboard, she pulled her portable CD player out of the junk drawer in the kitchen. She seldom used it, because she didn't like the earphones. But today she wanted a break from the racket Eddie was making downstairs.

She absently grabbed a quilt from the linen closet, realizing after she settled at the kitchen table that this was the quilt her mother made in celebration of her marriage to Walt. Mama had used a double wedding ring pattern—the same one Lela would have used for Darcie's quilt. She'd been married to Walt for three months when her mother presented the quilt. *Maybe I should've made that quilt for Darcie, even if I gave it to her three months late.*

She wrapped the quilt around her shoulders, feeling enfolded also in the memories of her forty-nine years with

Walt—the sweet, the bitter. When the tears came to her eyes in remembrance of an argument she had with Walter the week before he died, she knew that she needed something—anything—to take her mind off that track.

A glance at the Scripture sheet revealed the next passage to be read as Luke 1:39–56—Mary's visit to Elizabeth and Mary's song of praise. Lela winced. She felt anything but full of praise at that moment, especially at the thought of her upcoming furnace bill. She decided to listen to the announcement of Jesus' upcoming birth once again.

While she listened to the actors' dramatic reading of Mary's conversation with the angel Gabriel, her eyes strayed to the nine-block baby quilt pattern that had struck her the other day. Had she left the magazine open to this page? *Thought I closed it.* But as she gazed at the pattern once more, she suddenly knew: this is the one.

Guess it couldn't hurt to start piecing the top together. Might as well put that fabric to good use.

"Now, let's see. What do we have here?" She adjusted her glasses and peered at the pattern, only having to resort to the magnifier she kept by her Bible once or twice. Even

though the pattern called for red, yellow, orange, and green cottons, maybe she *could* make the colors she had—tan, peacock blue, cranberry, and cream—work with the baby quilt pattern. Well, they would have to do. She heaved a sigh of resignation. Already the quilt was starting to form in her mind, each roughly nine-inch block standing in sharp relief. I don't know who this is for, but I guess God knows. And, because it would be smaller, she would have material left over.

The first block called for a beach ball. She could use the blue fabric and add stripes out of the tan fabric—one of Walter's old dress shirts. She couldn't bring herself to look at it a year ago, but time had indeed healed some of the pain.

After retrieving the tote bag, she traced the simple shape on the blue cotton fabric—one of two fabrics purchased for the quilt. "Something old, something new, something borrowed, something blue" was the rule she followed while planning the wedding ring quilt, just as Mama taught her. The other purchase had been the cream background fabric. Well, it would have to serve for the baby quilt.

"How will this be?" a woman's voice suddenly blared from the CD.

Lela jumped, finally tuning in to the verses being read. The first part of Mary's question almost seemed to fit her thoughts about making a quilt. *How will this quilt come to be, seeing as how I don't usually make baby quilts? How will this quilt come to be, if I don't know who the quilt is for?*

"How will this be, since I am a virgin?" the actress playing Mary continued.

Ah. Those words seemed to hold not only human curiosity at the impossibility of conceiving a child without a man, but also the promise of a tide of misunderstandings and judgments that the event would cause in the future. How could she have a baby without a father? How could she survive if others—especially her fiancé, Joseph—gossiped about her and concluded that she had committed adultery? How could she bear the shame others would ascribe to the child's birth? But yet God called her to this impossible task at the very time when life held so much promise. Bearing his son was the mark of his favor.

Lela turned back to the quilt pattern. Was making this

quilt a task God had given her? If so, she didn't feel favored either. And the smiling sun and the other bright objects on the quilt pattern seemed far too cheerful for the way her life was going right now.

Maybe that was how the birth announcement seemed to Mary—a mixed blessing. Pregnancy is the best news a woman can receive, at least if it comes at a time when she is ready. Mary was willing to get ready, to deal with the circumstances being pregnant would bring, and even welcomed them, if it meant putting God's plan into motion.

Lela grunted. *Is that my cue to welcome this task?* She nodded to the block she had already begun to piece together.

Eddie bounded up the stairs. "Got the blower working for you. You should be good to go, Mrs. Edwards."

"Thanks."

He plunked a clipboard on the granite counter and wrote busily on it. She was soon presented with the results—the bill.

"Four hundred and fifty dollars!"

"Sorry. Merry Christmas. Uh, we also take Visa or MasterCard."

Lela grumbled under her breath as she grudgingly wrote the check. Merry Christmas indeed . . . $450.

Mary's "How will this be" ran through her mind. *How will this be, seeing as how I'm on a fixed income and money doesn't grow on trees?*

Well, at least the heat would be back on soon.

"Might take a little while to warm up in here," Eddie warned.

"That'll give me time to sort out a few things." Going back to Barbara's to coax Smokey back into his carrier would probably take another hour. She didn't relish the thought.

Barbara talked Lela into staying through dinner, reminding her that time was needed to allow the house to warm up. So she didn't reach home until around eight thirty that evening. Smokey yowled from his carrier in competition with the madly ringing phone as they entered the pleasantly warm house. Smokey was the winner, because the phone stopped before he did.

Just about a minute later, the doorbell rang. A quick look

through the peephole showed two police officers. She recognized one—the African American from the previous day. This time he was partnered with a slender Asian woman. Both had an almost comical look of surprise when she opened the door.

"We're sorry to disturb you, ma'am, but we have to check out all the calls we get . . ." He looked a little sheepish.

From his carrier, Smokey yowled in response, attracting the officers' full attention. "Is there a problem?" she asked. Had someone broken into her garage again? Or was this James again exercising his dialing finger by calling the police?

"Do you have a daughter named Jean Marshall?" the female officer asked.

Her heart thudded. "Yes. Did something happen to her?"

"She called about *you*. Apparently, she was worried about you and said she hadn't heard from you in over twenty-four hours."

"Oh." First the SSA thinking she was dead and now the police. Although she was hardly a blushing woman, Lela could feel the heat of embarrassment. She had forgotten to

check her messages! "As you can see, I'm fine. I spent the night at a neighbor's because my furnace wasn't working."

Smokey began yowling again as if in agreement.

"Guess your daughter was just worried about you," said the officer, after an exchanged glance with her partner. "I can't blame her. I worry about my mother sometimes."

"Maybe you should call your daughter," her partner chimed in. "Take it easy now."

Take it easy? Lela felt anything but easy as she slammed the door. She opened the carrier and watched Smokey shoot out, then checked the voicemail messages. There were several from Jean, two from Frank, and one from their brother Obadiah, who was the oldest now—had been as of five years ago when their brother Josiah died.

Jean's messages seemed more and more frantic. *Why is she so worried about me now?* There had been a time a few months ago when Jean barely called once a week. Now she was calling every day while Tamara and Sylvie called less.

Well, *she* could call *them*. She dialed Tamara's number.

Tamara picked up on the first ring. "Mama, what's going on over there? I just got a condolence letter from the SSA

telling me you're dead, and then Jean said she had to call the police on you."

"Tam, your sister overreacted. I'm fine. I spent the night at Barbara's, because the furnace wasn't working."

"And you couldn't pick up a phone to let someone know where you were?"

Lela flashed back to at least three instances when she had used that same phrase with Tam—all during her teen years when Tam hung out with her friends and forgot to call to say she was going to be late. Those were pre–cell phone days. But that was no excuse. Now she was just as without an excuse as Tam had been but didn't want to admit it. "I've had my hands full, Tamara. Anyway, I don't want you girls worrying about me. Just because someone tried to break into the garage—"

"Someone broke into the garage?"

Wait, hadn't she told them about it? She suddenly wished she hadn't said anything. "Tried to," she said. "I think it was the thirteen-year-old from across the street. He's always walking around like he owns the pla—"

A click in the line interrupted the conversation.

"I gotta take this, Mama. Hold on."

But soon the line clicked dead. Sighing, Lela hung up the phone.

Smokey rubbed himself against Lela's leg just as Tamara rang back. "Sorry. Client emergency. I've gotta run."

"At this time of night?"

"Mama, just because it's almost Christmas, that doesn't mean I'm on vacation. This case goes to trial right after Christmas. I've still gotta be prepared. Anyway, you really need to think about moving. The neighborhood's getting bad. Aren't there some crackheads living on Justine? That's just a block away. Think about it."

She hung up before Lela could get another word in edge-wise. Lela liked to be the one with the last word.

Just as she dialed Sylvie's number, the doorbell rang. She hung up the phone. Deborah from the corner house across the street was at the door. Now what does she want? An apology for the loud music a few nights ago seemed a long shot. Lela flicked on the porch light and opened the door a crack.

Deborah wore an odd mixture of clothes—a pumpkin

fleece vest over a black dress with a short hemline, black panty hose, a red wool hat, and thick-soled brown shoes that definitely didn't go with the dress—as if she had dressed in haste or in a very dark room.

"You haven't seen Ronnie around, have you?"

Lela stared at her. Now why was she asking that? Lela didn't keep track of the boy's whereabouts.

"He said he was going to the park, but he was supposed to be back by now."

"I saw him yesterday but haven't seen him at all today." What Lela didn't say aloud was *I'd better not catch him around here. I know he's the one that stole that bath oil. And what is she doing letting him wander the streets at all hours of the day or night?*

Yet the look on Deborah's face—worry veering toward desperation—was starting to get to her. She didn't want to pity her, didn't want to invite her in out of the cold as if they were on friendly terms.

"I just . . . I just don't know what to do with that boy sometimes. He's a good kid—"

Lela snorted. That was what they all said, usually followed

by the "My child would never do such a thing" speech that Al Capone's mama probably used all the while he was on a murdering spree. "It's kinda late for him to be out in the streets, isn't it?"

The look of worry was suddenly replaced with a defiant look. "Sorry to disturb you." Deborah hurried down the stairs and headed south toward Barbara's end of the block at a fast pace.

Lela closed the door, suddenly regretting her words. *Well, someone had to say something.* As she picked up Smokey, who stood at her feet yowling for attention, she was haunted by a nagging sense that she needed to do something about Ronnie. But what could she do? She needed to assure her *own* family of her safety.

Sylvie's line was busy. *Jean. I need to call Jean.* She felt a twinge of relief mixed with guilt, however, when she received a busy signal.

She flipped on the TV in time to catch a Christmas movie—the perfect thing to quilt by. But just as she reached for her work bag, the phone rang.

"Mother, what's going on?" asked Jean. "I've been calling and calling and calling—"

"And calling the police, I see. They came by the house."

"I was worried when you didn't answer the phone. It was only after I called the police that I talked to Mrs. Wiggins. She told me you stayed down there. She also said someone broke into your garage."

"I meant to call you back, but one thing after another happened today. Oh, and I stopped at the Social Security office yesterday too, trying to straighten out this mess. But just because I don't answer the phone, that doesn't mean you have to call the police!"

Jean finally spoke after a few moments of silence. "I was thinking about Great-aunt Joelle."

Oh no, she didn't! *She* would *have to go there.* Lela's anger flared. "Your great-aunt was *senile,* Jeanette Marie, and *stuck* in her bathtub! That's no reason to suddenly think *I've* gone senile!"

"Mother, I was *worried,* that's all. You need to take it easy sometimes. Did you eat dinner?"

Lela sighed. Why did this child know how to push her buttons? "Now you're worried that I'm forgetting to eat? Of course I ate! Do you want to know *what* I ate?"

"Mother, why do you always have to start a fight? I'm just asking."

Lela longed to change the subject. "How's everybody there?"

"Your son-in-law's out Christmas shopping. You got the presents we sent, right?"

"Under the tree."

"You should open the one with the blue wrapping paper. Joelle made you some of her fudge. "

Joelle was Jean's youngest daughter, named for Great-aunt Joelle. Lela gritted her teeth at the reminder of Joelle.

"Blue wrapping paper. Okay. I'll open it as soon as I get off the phone."

"I can take a hint, Mother. I'll talk to you later, then."

As soon as she hung up, Lela retrieved the present from underneath the tree, suddenly realizing that she hadn't finished placing the ornaments on the branches. Some still lay in boxes on the end table. She shook her head. How had she forgotten to do that? The excitement of the last two days had thrown her off.

She wished Darcie were coming. She knew how to make a tree beautiful.

She sighed as she stood by the window, gazing at the blinking array of Christmas decorations at the house directly across from hers. The house was covered in acres of blue, red, and green Christmas lights. And that house competed with *its* next-door neighbor's giant Christmas stars in five different gaudy flashing colors.

Now who was that standing on the edge of her lawn? She squinted at the figure. Ronnie? Was he peeping through her window? No. Just standing there, his arms raised. There was something about his posture that suddenly reminded her of her daughters when they were small, out there catching snowflakes on their tongues. But what was the boy doing standing on her snow-covered lawn?

She marched to the door and threw it open. "Boy, get off my lawn and go on home to your mama! She's out looking for you!"

But Ronnie ran off in the opposite direction from his house.

Lela shook her head as she dialed Barbara's number. Not for the first time did she wonder if the boy was a little simple in the head. "If Deborah shows up around your house,

tell her I saw Ronnie," she said, just as Barbara said hello.

"She was just by here. I'll tell her if I see her. Or you can call her yourself. I'll give you her cell phone number."

"Just tell her, would you?" She hung up before Barbara could talk her into calling Deborah. She'd done her duty. Surely that was enough.

ela took her usual place behind the second pillar at the back of the sanctuary on Sunday morning.

The sanctuary comfortably seated one thousand—just under half of their twenty-five-hundred-member congregation. This was the second service and, as usual, was filled beyond capacity. Among the overflow were visitors who usually only darkened the doorway of a church at Christmas and Easter.

Cream and red poinsettias lined the pulpit stage, while purple and gold banners proclaiming the birth of Christ festooned the walls near the large, intricately carved cross at center stage behind the pastors' chairs.

Lela wore the black suit that constituted the usher's uniform. In honor of the season, they added a purple and gold

scarf, but she could never get hers to hang just right. Even now the scarf listed to the left, almost as if she had a tourniquet over her left shoulder.

The choir processed in singing "Nearer My God to Thee"—not exactly what Lela expected for the season. But the atmosphere was uplifting nonetheless. As usual, there was an air of expectancy in the congregation, as they waited for the message. Lela wondered what Pastor would preach about—something more in keeping with Christmas than the processional hymn.

The choir now sang a version of a Yolanda Adams song, "What About the Children?"—another surprising choice for the season. As they finished, the senior pastor, Richard Davis, got up to speak, bringing with him a large Bible, with loose pages that flopped about with a life of their own. Davis was tall—about six feet six—and had the kind of smooth, even, caramel skin that many women wish they had. Lela noted with approval that he had shaved off the beard he'd been wearing recently.

"Now, I know it's Christmas and y'all want to hear the Christmas story," he began, showing his Texas roots by his

intonation. "But I feel led today to talk from Matthew nineteen, thirteen to fifteen. Yes, many of us have heard the story of parents bringing their children to Jesus to be blessed. But I want to challenge us today about whether or not we're bringing children to him. Not just *our* children but grandchildren, or even our neighbors' children." He seemed to look around at everyone present.

Lela squirmed, wondering why he seemed to look at her.

"Now, Christmas is all about Jesus, all about his coming to serve as a tiny baby. Our kids will remind us of that when they get up here in a week and do their thing." The congregation remarked and chuckled, knowing exactly what the pastor meant. "Christmas is a reminder that Mary's baby came to save the children of this world. Now, we're all somebody's child, aren't we?"

Some in the congregation said "Amen" and "Preach, brother."

"Now, I hear that some of you ladies have been reading in your Bible study sessions lately about Mary. You recall the story of how Mary and Joseph presented Jesus in the temple out of obedience to the law of Moses found in Leviticus.

As their firstborn child, Jesus was dedicated to God's service. That story is also a reminder to us to bring our children and our neighbors' children to the Lord to fulfill his law of love."

More "Amens" issued from the people. Lela flinched as if struck. She now recalled Deborah's look of desperation the other night as she searched for her child. She hadn't even prayed for Deborah or for Ronnie, and the realization pierced her heart.

Just before the offertory, the choir launched into a jazzy rendition of "What Child Is This?" Lela's eyes suddenly filled with tears. Now, why was she thinking about that no-good Ronnie standing in the snow with his arms raised as if waiting for someone to pick him up and tell him that everything was going to be okay? Why did she suddenly think that that someone should have been her?

She suddenly wished she had taken Barbara up on her offer that morning to switch Sundays with her and go with some of the senior women to the nursing home. In this moment, she would rather have been there than here.

She sighed and surreptitiously brushed away the tears as she followed her section partner, Philip, in passing the offering baskets.

"Lela, you okay?" Philip whispered as they processed out of the sanctuary with the offering. "You just passed the plate to a B row. You never do that."

"Sorry. My mind was elsewhere."

For the first time ever, she couldn't wait for the service to end.

Now that the streets were clear, Lela felt safe enough to drive the Camry on the Tri-State and Route 394. She was headed the twenty-five miles out to Crete to Frank's.

Normally, the drive through wooded areas was a pretty and pleasant one. But with the roads still somewhat winter slick, her heart was in her mouth. She kept a watch for stray deer as she drove along the tree-lined road and descended the small hill to loop around to Frank's road, Norway Trail. She was relieved when she saw the front of Frank's two-story colonial.

As usual, the Christmas decorations showed the war between taste and tastelessness. She could almost pinpoint who in Frank's family made which contribution. An army of candy canes littered the grass at the right of the long

driveway. Frank's grandchildren, Lela guessed. A Santa with a peeling brown face waited with a loaded sleigh on the snow-covered lawn next to a manger scene: Frank's contribution. He was always sentimental about dragging out the old decorations, even those from the 1970s. The bottom fourth of the pine tree on the edge of the drive held three ribbons of white Christmas lights. Rhoda's contribution—an attempt at bringing in some taste.

Lela tried to imagine what the decorations would have been like if Frank's first wife, Gia, had survived cancer. She would've allowed the kids to have greater say in the decorating, probably. At the front door, a deer made of lights (Rhoda too, probably) had blown over next to the porch.

As Frank opened the door, grinning from ear to ear, she felt a blast of welcoming warmth and music that assaulted. Must be the kids upstairs blasting some kind of Christmas song mix from a CD player or one of those iPods. She also heard a tide of voices rising in the family room.

"Glad you could make it, Le." Frank kissed her cheek and helped her off with her coat in the foyer. At five eight, he was only a couple of inches taller than she, so they were nearly eye level.

All her brothers, with the exception of Samuel, called her by her middle name or the shortened form of her first name, Le.

"Cee Cee's here with Vaughn," Frank continued. "And the grandkids are upstairs wrapping gifts." The grandchildren were courtesy of Rhoda's oldest son.

"With music playing that loudly, I think the neighbors know they're here."

Frank chuckled, but Lela caught a shadow of worry in the brown eyes that were so like hers—like Mama's really, she thought. Something was up.

"It's been a while since I've seen my niece." Cee Cee, or Catherine, was twenty-five years old. *Where has the time gone?* Lela said to herself.

"And Rhoda's cousin Bud and Angela came through from the West Side. You should've let them pick you up. You wouldn't have had to drive."

"You know I live too far out of their way."

"They don't mind, seriously. Well, come on in. I'm glad you're here. Need to talk to you about something, Le. Didn't wanna tell you over the phone."

"Wanna talk now or after dinner?"

"Later."

Lela nodded and moved toward the dining room. As usual, there were people at every turn in Frank's house This was Frank in his element—surrounded by family. And the house with its open floor plan put them all on display.

His mother-in-law, Ida, who now lived with them, sat alone at the table in the dining room, next to her walker. Lela grasped the wrinkled hand of the ninety-year-old, receiving a soft squeeze in return. "How are you today, Miss Ida?" she said loudly, as Ida was hard of hearing.

"I feel pretty good, pretty good, thank the good Lord," Ida said softly. "How you feel, young lady?"

"I guess I can't complain." At least not at the unexpected bonus of being called "young lady," Lela thought. Unlike Frank, she didn't have any parents-in-law around to make her feel young. Walt's mother had died of cancer when they were married only three years. His ninety-four-year-old father lived in a nursing facility in Louisville, Kentucky, where many of Walt's relatives still lived. He hadn't known who she was, the last time she visited, thanks to Alzheimer's. He'd been very friendly, unlike how he had been when his memory was intact.

In the large kitchen across the hall from the dining room, her sister-in-law Rhoda labored to pull a turkey out of the oven. Unlike Frank's first wife, Rhoda wasn't a touchy-feely hugger. She was usually content, as she seemed now, with a "Hey, girl. Come on in." As usual, she looked exhausted. Had probably cooked for days and would be too tired to eat.

Lela again nodded a greeting and went to the family room to see who else had arrived. Her sixty-year-old cousin Lance, who lived on the West Side, sat on the love seat with a pretty young woman approximately half his age. She could only assume, from the girl's vacuous look, that this was his latest girlfriend. And there was Angela on the couch next to her husband, Rhoda's cousin Bud, who was asleep already. A football game blared from the large, flat-screened TV on the wall above the fireplace. Lela couldn't tell which teams were playing, nor did she care. Baseball and basketball were her games.

"Hey, Lela!" Lance called, finally tearing himself away from the game. And no wonder. Commercial break. "Did you hear that Cousin Russell died?"

"No. Nobody told me Russell died." Suddenly Lela felt

tired and fragile. Russell was ten years younger and supposedly robust.

"Yeah, just yesterday. Aneurysm. Who knew? Funeral's probably gonna be next week. You going down to Mississippi with us?"

"You're asking, when I just heard this minute about it."

"Let her get in good before you start going on about Russell," said Frank.

"Did you bring peach cobbler?" asked Lance.

"I'm sorry I didn't cook anything," Lela said, throwing a look at Rhoda in the kitchen. "I came straight here after church."

"Girl, we got tons of food," said Rhoda, waving to the stove, where pots steamed and bubbled. Lela could smell the greens and the cinnamon of the sweet potatoes. "Sit yourself down, if you can find room."

There was no room on the couch or the love seat. Lela eased herself down at the end of the table in the large kitchen, where she could still see everyone in the family room. She was feeling a twinge in her shoulder. She would have to take some ibuprofen as soon as she got some food in her stomach.

She gazed at the decorations on the table. Like its twin in the dining room, it had been elegantly set for the meal with Christmas china and gold flatware. The only incongruous items among the elegant dinnerware were the decorated green plastic cups. Each had some type of construction paper tree or ornament glued to it.

"My grandbaby made those." Rhoda looked proud.

Lela shook her head. The cups looked off balance, like they bore too much weight in the front. Surely they would fall over the moment anyone tried to fill them with liquid. "So where's Catherine?" she asked, wanting to change the subject.

"Out for a walk with Vaughn."

"It's gotta be thirty degrees outside."

"You know how young people are. Can't stay cooped up for long."

The door opened half an hour later and a young woman entered, brushing snow out of shoulder-length honey brown hair (the same brown as her aunt Sylvie's—probably used the same hair coloring) that should have been under a hat. Catherine had Frank's cinnamon complexion with a light dusting of freckles. But she had her mama's beauty.

"Well, finally, Miss Catherine Claudia. Come on over here and give your aunt a hug, Cee Cee."

"Hey, Aunt Lela," Cee Cee called, tugging on the hand of a tall young man with an abundance of curly black hair, almond-shaped eyes, and skin the color of honey. She released his hand long enough to give Lela a brief hug. She was quick enough to reclaim his hand. "Here's Vaughn."

As if she couldn't see him. He was what the young people called "hot"—a term she found vulgar, but which seemed appropriate in Vaughn's case.

"Pleased to meet you," he said in a well-modulated voice.

"Hello." Lela knew her voice sounded reserved. But no one instantly gained her favor. It was bestowed like a gift.

"Did you bring your peach cobbler? I told Vaughn you make the best peach cobbler."

"Girl, I ain't had no time in between church and coming here."

As Catherine and Vaughn joined the crush in the family room, Lela whispered to Rhoda about the boyfriend, "He ain't all the way black, is he?"

"He's not black at all. His mother's from Vietnam and

his dad's from Guatemala. His mother died a couple of years ago, though. Car accident."

Lela suddenly felt a twinge of sympathy "Is he a believer at least?"

"Wants to be a missionary overseas somewhere. I don't know how that'll work with Cee Cee, though. I'm not sure how she'll handle a missionary life. She's not used to roughing it. She doesn't even like to go camping."

Frank entered the kitchen, rubbing his hands together. "Everybody ready to eat?" he called in a voice sure to carry throughout the house.

There was a chorus of "Yes," "All right, now," and "About time," followed by the thump of feet running down stairs.

"Let's gather around the table so we can bless the food," Frank said. Everyone, including Frank's three grandchildren, made a ring around the table. Lela felt her hand clasped by Vaughn's warm hand.

As usual Frank prayed for a long while. Lela could hear the grandkids squirming as well as a few murmured sighs from the adults. But Frank seemed oblivious.

Finally, they were seated and the grabbing for food began

in earnest. Rhoda poured punch, then had to hastily mop the table as one green cup with a Christmas tree fell over. Lela stopped herself from saying, "I told you so."

All through dinner, she half listened to the conversation, as she watched Catherine and Vaughn. They hardly seemed to take their eyes off each other. They were in the bubble— the one people in love seemed to slip into, which insulates them against the sharp edges of life and makes everything rosy.

She suddenly felt a wave of sorrow for Darcie, remembering the Christmas when she brought Doug to Lela's. Both had looked just as desperately in love. Yet their bubble had been pierced. When had that love died? Did it die? What did happen with them? Would the love between Catherine and Vaughn last? Or would they later decide that a divorce was better than honoring their commitment?

Frank, who sat on her left, suddenly passed his hand in front of her face. "Le, what were you thinking so hard about?"

Lela blinked. "Oh. Sorry. I was thinking about Darcie."

Frank grunted. "Yeah, I heard. Sad."

"What's sad?" asked Lance.

Time to change the subject. The two had the same thought at the same time. "Feels funny not going home for Christmas this year," Lela said. The image of the big farmhouse built by their father rose in her mind, along with the smaller houses two of her brothers lived in just down the road apiece in Cannonsburg.

"It's not the same with Mama gone," said Frank.

Lela nodded, thinking of the cancer that took their ninety-two-year-old mother over a year ago—just a month before Darcie married. Six months after Walt. What a year that had been. What doesn't kill you can only make you stronger, they say. She herself was still alive, but certainly not stronger.

"Does that mean you're not going to Russell's funeral?" Lance looked as if that were the crime of the century.

"I don't think I'll make it—not this close to Christmas." Although with Darcie not coming, did she really have an excuse *not* to go?

Lela stood, helping to carry plates to the sink. She even volunteered to wash the china, still half listening to the ebb and flow of the conversations, feeling blessed for having a large family. The pastor's words about bringing children to

God came to mind, again. She couldn't help thinking of Deborah wandering around in the cold, looking for her son, and of later finding that son on her lawn.

"It's starting to snow out, Le," said Frank, from his perch by the sliding doors leading to the backyard. "Maybe you should stay over."

At that moment, music began to blare from upstairs, followed by the sound of several voices laughing and assorted thumps.

"Naw. Think I'll head on home. Thanks all the same."

"If you're through with those dishes, come on back here to the office."

Frank led her to a small room at the back of the house. Inside was a desktop computer on a small table in one corner; a cot and a small black leather loveseat took up much of the space otherwise.

Frank sat at the computer desk, leaving her the love seat. He seemed content to roll a pen back and forth on the desk, rather than speak.

"Prime the pump, Francis," said Lela. It was an old joke with them and a reminder of the old water pump on their farm growing up. He was raising the handle of his thoughts

up and down to get the words like water out. Frank flashed a smile shaped by concern. "I worry about you, sis, living out in the old neighborhood alone like you are. Maybe you should think about moving out this way. I can find you a house out here. It's quieter."

At that moment, a blast of music from upstairs belied his statement. "Well, you know what I mean. You need to get out of the city, sis."

Lela sighed. After a long pause, she asked, "If I were Oby or Barnabas, would we be having this conversation?"

Frank sighed and remained silent for a bit. "Maybe not. But with Walter gone, don't you get lonely?" He paused. "Maybe I'm thinking more like this now that Rhoda's mother has come to live with us. You don't have to do it all by yourself, taking care of a house."

"What else can I do if I'm a widow?" Lela said.

"Ever think about getting a smaller place? I can find you a condo out this way."

Lela suddenly thought about Mary. God had chosen her to bear his son. He'd given her Joseph as her husband. But Joseph probably died before Jesus became a man. She might have been a widow at a young age—a widow who had to raise

Jesus and his siblings on her own. Did she have to hear things like that—the concern of those who couldn't believe that a woman could make it without a man? It had to be worse for Mary, with mouths to feed in her house.

"Frank, I'm not ready to move right now. 'Preciate your concern though. I'll let you know if I change my mind."

"Sure you won't spend the night?"

Another blast of music from upstairs decided her. "Positive."

What do you mean you haven't straightened out this mess? I'm alive, aren't I? And standing right in front of you." She waved the letter she'd just received that Monday morning from her chatty mailman, Marc.

"Ma'am, we're doing the best we can," said the woman behind the counter at the Social Security office. This time, instead of the brown sweater, she had on a purple and gold-striped sweater that was, to Lela's mind, just as unflattering.

"Why would you send a letter to me if you thought I was dead?"

"The problem is we have to trace when the mistake was made and go from there."

Lela shook her head, turned on her heels, and left.

"Why do I bother coming to this office just to hear that?" Lela complained to Barbara, as they returned to the car.

Barbara shrugged. "I'm sure they're working on it. Feel up to making a detour? I want to get to Target on 118th and get a couple of things."

Lela didn't feel up to it, if truth be told. But it was nice of Barbara to drive. And perhaps she could do a little shopping. She didn't have much left to do—just a few trinkets to hand out at Bible study. She'd already sent cards to the grandchildren—with smaller amounts of money than she'd planned to give before the furnace broke down. She had yet to replace Darcie's stolen gift.

"Look, there's Deborah." Barbara waved to her at the cafeteria.

Lela thought, *Speak of the devil, or the mama of the devil* . . . Just as soon as the words formed in her mind, she felt rebuked by the Holy Spirit.

Barbara grabbed a shopping cart. "Do you see how awful she looks? Did you know she kicked Leo out?"

"How would I know that? It's not like she tells me her business. We hardly ever talk."

"You didn't hear what happened? Eileen said she could hear him screaming at her from outside, some kind of fighting going on. James called the police again, but Leo left before they came."

"When did *that* happen?"

"Yesterday evening."

She silently praised God that Frank had invited her to his house for dinner. "Huh." She glanced back at Deborah, who was now helping a customer.

Barbara sighed, then took a quick look to the right and to the left as if afraid of being overheard. "She threw his stuff in the yard and changed the locks on him. He didn't take it too well."

"Good riddance, I say. But what made her do it? Was he beating on her?"

Barbara shrugged. "Probably. I think it has something to do with Ronnie. She's been having a rough time with him lately."

"That's what happens when you don't raise children properly," Lela said.

Barbara responded with a look that suggested she wanted

to say something. But she closed her mouth instead and shook her head.

Lela folded her arms. "You got something to say?"

"I need to go to electronics. Can I meet you by the cafeteria in twenty minutes?"

Fifteen minutes later, after she'd sought and not found what she needed in the health and beauty section, Lela's sore feet prompted her to sit on the bench outside the cafeteria.

"Can I get you something?" Deborah called over. "Some water or something?"

"No, thank you." She knew that her voice sounded cold, but she couldn't inject any warmth into it. She was thankful when Barbara soon wandered over and asked, "How are you holding up?"

Before she could answer, Lela realized that Barbara's question was to Deborah.

"Okay. I think Ronnie's glad Leo's gone. They never got along. Leo never really understood Ronnie. Thought I babied him too much. But the doctor keeps switching his medication, which makes him a little hard to deal with sometimes, especially when he can't get to sleep."

Barbara nodded sympathetically. "He's ADHD, right?"

Deborah nodded. She glanced away as a tall man in a red shirt suddenly loomed near a display case filled with sandwiches. "Uh-oh. Shift manager. Gotta get back to work."

Lela shook her head as they walked back to the car. "It sounds like she's lost control over the boy."

"I think she's afraid someone might report her to CPS," said Barbara. "But she's a hard worker."

"Is something wrong with him?"

"You just heard me say he's ADHD."

"Yeah, but they diagnose most kids with that nowadays. And they're not all running around the neighborhood wild. I saw him a few days ago, standing in the middle of my lawn like he owned it or something. I gave him what for."

Barbara shrugged, as she backed out of the space at a speed that caused Lela to clutch the armrest. "He seems lonely. And I think the boyfriend was abusive. That's probably why she kicked him out."

Lela squelched her desire to comment on women who

always seemed to pick abusive men. None of *her* sons-in-law hit their wives. Deborah's life was already sounding like several episodes of a bad talk show. "Why don't any of her family help?" she asked instead.

"As far as I know, her mama doesn't have much to do with her. I don't think she's quite right in the head. Deborah's mama, that is. And the dad's not in the picture."

"Why does that not surprise me?"

"At least she's trying to take care of her son."

"I still think he stole my bag out of your car."

"We don't know that. I think he deserves a second chance, especially at Christmas, don't you?"

"What is this, one of those Christmas movies on Lifetime? Give the kid a break and it'll be just the Christmas miracle he needs to straighten out? Some kids just turn out bad, Barbara. Give him a break and you'll just encourage him or his friends to steal more than just a lawn mower or a Christmas gift."

"He *deserves* mercy."

Lela glanced out of the window, thinking back to Pastor Davis's message on Sunday. She began to feel the reprimanding hand of the Spirit. "I will pray for Ronnie," Lela said

aloud grudgingly, "but I don't know if it will do any good for someone like him."

The phone rang just as Lela returned home. As soon as she picked up, Sylvie said impatiently, "Mama, what's all this about—?"

"I'm alive and it's all a mistake at the Social Security office."

"Obviously." Sylvie laughed. "Where you been? I called you earlier."

"I didn't get a message."

"I called your cell. Don't you ever answer it?"

"You know I don't like using it. Anyway, I was out shopping with Barbara."

"By the way, I brought your Christmas gifts with me to the in-laws. They said hi, by the way. We'll open them on Christmas Eve."

"I wish you were coming home this Christmas. It's going to be a lonely Christmas here."

"What do you mean? I thought Darcie was coming."

"Didn't Jean tell you? She's not coming. She's getting divorced instead."

"Mama . . ."

"I'm just telling it the way your sister told me."

"I'm sure there's more to it than that. Was it Doug again? Jean said they were having some problems."

"Well, problem solved now. Divorce is the answer."

"That's pretty harsh, Mama. . . . Poor Darcie. Where is she, by the way, if she's not coming there?"

"Going to your sister's."

"Probably wanted to be near her mama. You can't blame her. I'm gonna call over there in a minute. Just thought I'd check on you. Are you getting Tamara to check on this SSA business?"

"She seemed a little rushed last week."

"Whoops. And here I am, having to rush off too. I'm sorry, Mama. I'll check on you later."

Before she could say a word, Sylvie had hung up. Lela stared at the phone, wondering how time with her daughters had suddenly boiled down to a few hasty conversations on the phone.

I could use a good word. Instead of picking up her piece-work, she picked up the Bible and turned to Luke 1, to read the first passage of Scripture on the sheet: Luke 1:26–38, the

birth announcement. More and more, as the days passed, she felt drawn to that story.

LUKE 1:26–38

And in the sixth month the angel Gabriel was sent from God unto a city of Galilee, named Nazareth, to a virgin espoused to a man whose name was Joseph, of the house of David; and the virgin's name was Mary. And the angel came in unto her, and said, Hail, thou that art highly favored, the Lord is with thee: blessed art thou among women. And when she saw him, she was troubled at his saying, and cast in her mind what manner of salutation this should be. And the angel said unto her, Fear not, Mary: for thou hast found favor with God. And, behold, thou shalt conceive in thy womb, and bring forth a son, and shalt call his name JESUS. He shall be great, and shall be called the Son of the Highest: and the Lord God shall give unto him the throne of his father David: and he shall reign over the house of Jacob for ever; and of his kingdom there shall be no end. Then said Mary unto the angel, How shall this be, seeing I know not a man? And the angel answered and said unto her, The Holy Ghost

shall come upon thee, and the power of the Highest shall
overshadow thee: therefore also that holy thing which
shall be born of thee shall be called the Son of God. And,
behold, thy cousin Elisabeth, she hath also conceived a son
in her old age; and this is the sixth month with her, who
was called barren. And the angel departed from her.

Lela imagined how Mary praised God, despite the uncertainty of her life, despite the fact that she might lose Joseph, lose the respect of her community, or be branded an immoral woman—all because she chose to say yes to God.

One section of Mary's song of praise nearly leaped off the large-print page:

Luke 1:54, 55

He hath holpen his servant Israel, in remembrance of
his mercy; as he spake to our fathers, to Abraham, and to
his seed for ever.

Humph. Barbara talked about mercy earlier. But surely that couldn't mean—

The tinkle of breaking glass interrupted the thought. She

hurried into the living room and saw a litter of broken ornaments under the tree.

"Smokey!" She had forgotten how irresistible ornaments on a Christmas tree were to a cat. Knowing him, he was probably under the couch or the overstuffed chair by the door. He'd probably stay there for hours, hiding from her wrath. She sighed, now wishing she had daughters here, instead of a cat who broke ornaments and cost her a bundle in food and vet bills. And now if he managed to cut himself on the broken glass . . .

With a sigh, she retrieved the dustpan, then with a pained grunt knelt under the tree. It was almost as if Smokey knew just the right ornaments to break: some of her favorites. Sylvie had given her the two red glass ornaments with angels on them. And Jean had given her the Waterford crystal snowflake—saved up her money from her first job at the age of seventeen to pay for it. Now all three were in pieces on the floor—her fault for putting them so low on the tree.

As she scooped up the shards, Mary's praise for God's mercy played over and over in her mind, along with Barbara's

insistence that Ronnie be shown mercy. Mary willingly acknowledged God's mercy, all the while contemplating how drastically her life was about to change. Would it be smashed irretrievably like the ornaments? For all she knew, at the time, it might have been. But instead of complaining, she offered praise.

Lela's mind turned to Deborah and the look on her face on the night she came to her house in search of Ronnie. Her life seemed shattered too. *Her fault too.*

She returned to the kitchen table and her Bible. *"He hath holpen his servant Israel, in remembrance of his mercy,"* she read again.

At that moment, a penitent-looking Smokey crept down the hallway. His tail curled around his feet as he sat by the table, as if unsure of his welcome.

She grunted. "Just like a man. You break something and then act as if nothing happened. Get over here, boy."

But Smokey stayed where he was.

"Guess I have to come to you." Lela shook her head as she crossed to him and scooped him up. He settled against her shoulder, purring, as if relieved that she'd made the first

move. He was fine, not even a cut paw. "You're a mess, you know that?"

She couldn't help wondering if she needed to make the first move with Ronnie also. She shook her head, dismissing the thought.

a'am, we're *still* working on the mistake."

Lela sighed as she hung up the phone. She didn't have to call or go by there every day. But it made her feel better to be doing something about the situation.

MATTHEW 1:18–25

Now the birth of Jesus Christ was on this wise: When as his mother Mary was espoused to Joseph, before they came together, she was found with child of the Holy Ghost. Then Joseph her husband, being a just man, and not willing to make her a public example, was minded to put her away privily. But while he thought on these things, behold, the angel of the Lord appeared unto him in a dream, saying,

Joseph, thou son of David, fear not to take unto thee Mary thy wife: for that which is conceived in her is of the Holy Ghost. And she shall bring forth a son, and thou shalt call his name JESUS: for he shall save his people from their sins. Now all this was done, that it might be fulfilled which was spoken of the Lord by the prophet, saying, Behold, a virgin shall be with child, and shall bring forth a son, and they shall call his name Immanuel, which being interpreted is, God with us. Then Joseph being raised from sleep did as the angel of the Lord had bidden him, and took unto him his wife: And knew her not till she had brought forth her firstborn son: and he called his name JESUS.

The third passage to read was Matthew 1:18–25—an angel appearing to Joseph in a dream. After turning on the CD player, Lela settled at the table to piece together the second and third blocks of the quilt: a baby's foot on a red background and a cranberry heart on a blue background.

Piecework was her favorite part of making a quilt. She loved cutting out shapes and figuring out how they might work together.

Maybe that was how Joseph felt—like he didn't know

how life would work out in the face of Mary's startling and devastating news. The child Mary carried wasn't *his* child. He had to wonder if Mary cheated on him. That was only natural. A woman had to have a man in order to conceive a child. Despite his suspicions of betrayal, he thought perhaps he could do right by Mary, in his mind, by divorcing her quietly.

Divorce.

Darcie.

She'd never really connected Darcie's situation with Joseph's before. Evidently, she didn't think she could ever trust Doug again.

Joseph agreed to stand by Mary in the end, but he didn't fully understand the situation. Even after the angel told him of God's involvement in the conception of Jesus, did he wonder if he could ever fully trust her again? Did he struggle to accept the son Mary later bore? The Bible didn't say. It *did* say that he was immediately obedient and took Mary home as his wife. Perhaps his obedience revealed enough of his character.

She missed Walt with a fierceness that caused her to set her piecework on the table and go in search of the photo

albums again—the ones with the black-and-white photos from way back when.

She slowly flipped through the pictures. There was Walt standing by Alice Tanner Hall—her dormitory at Alcorn Agricultural and Mechanical College, Alcorn State University now. This was at the end of his sophomore year and her freshman year. She'd liked him the first moment she saw him striding across the library. He was—as the kids today would say—hot back in 1958 at the age of twenty-one, with that slow, cocky smile, the hazel eyes he passed only to Jean, and a slight resemblance to Smokey Robinson in his prime. Although not the tallest man (five nine in his stockinged feet), he gave the impression of height by sheer attitude. She couldn't remember who took that picture. One of his friends or hers perhaps?

Wasn't *this* the day that he finally declared that he liked her not just as a friend, but as someone he wanted to go steady with? *Go steady.* No one used that term these days. She had worn a purple dress that day. Or was it pink? The memory was getting fuzzier and fuzzier.

Although Mama and Daddy liked Walt, they hadn't wanted her to marry Walt before they finished college. But by the end of her sophomore year, she thought she would absolutely *die* if

she didn't marry him. They made the big step after her junior year. She barely finished college before Tamara was born.

Maybe Mary loved Joseph this way—as someone she couldn't imaging living without. He was quite a bit older than her—or so Lela had heard over the years at church—unlike Walter, who was only a year older than her. Was Mary frightened at the thought that she might not be able to marry him, that he might not accept her son as his own? That he might cling to the belief that she cheated on him?

Or perhaps she never knew just how close she came to being divorced quietly, as Matthew 1:19 mentioned. Because of the angel's message in the dream, perhaps he continued to look forward instead of giving her sidelong looks with a residue of mistrust.

Walter had never cheated on her. That she knew for sure. But she couldn't say she always understood him or vice versa, especially during the rocky periods in their marriage—one coming right after Tamara was born. Money was tight, and it seemed like both their tempers were permanently short. And she'd gone through a bad bout of what everyone nowadays called postpartum depression. Back then she just thought she was overwhelmed by the new responsibilities of a baby. It

was only by the grace of God that their marriage survived *that* storm.

So why couldn't Darcie's? Perhaps Doug had stretched Darcie's understanding to the breaking point.

The phone suddenly rang, startling her out of her reverie. She glanced at the clock. Eleven thirty. Over an hour had passed since she begun looking at the photos.

"Feel up to more Christmas shopping?" asked Barbara.

"You're always out in the streets these days."

"'Tis the season. I still need to get a few last-minute angel tree gifts. I might also get something for Ronnie."

Lela snorted. "Didn't he get enough out of your car and Eileen's garage?"

Barbara sighed. "We don't know that he's the one doing it. There *are* some gang members around the 'hood. Anyway, I feel sorry for that boy."

"Can't his mama get him something? It's her fault he's running around like he is, disrespecting his elders. It's all that music they're listening to nowadays."

Barbara sighed. "Are you coming or not?"

"Well, I still never replaced Darcie's gift. Where are you getting these few last-minute angel tree gifts?"

"Does it matter? Are you up to anything right now?"

"Well, I've been working on that quilt you nagged me about making. I felt conflicted about it."

"Wonderful. Gonna donate it to angel tree?"

"Maybe. I don't really know. I just know I need to do it."

"What else you got going on?"

Lela almost laughed. What *did* she have going on? Life certainly wasn't like that old TV show, *The Golden Girls,* with a man around every corner or some kind of conflict neatly solved in half an hour. Sometimes life was simply mundane. "Gotta get the washing done. It's piling up downstairs."

"Knowing you, you probably scheduled all of your activities for the next three months. You probably need to get outta the house. After shopping, let's stop at Dock's. I need me some catfish."

"I thought you said your cholesterol was high."

"I'll be there in five minutes."

Lela was relieved when they headed to Kohl's, rather than Barbara's usual store of choice, Target. She was also relieved

that Barbara drove, as she watched the flick and flutter of snow flurries dotting the gray sky.

"I want to stop over at the baby department and look at a few things," Barbara announced in the store, but she immediately halted by a rack of jeans. "Ooh, here are those jeans they talked about on *Oprahs.*"

Again with the plurals, Lela mused with a shake of the head.

Barbara fingered a pair of jeans that Lela was certain she couldn't get into with a shoehorn and a million years of hoping. She finally pulled Barbara away from the rack and toward the baby department.

"Don't tell me Sidney's wife's expecting again." She decided not to add the fact that Sidney was also unemployed, yet still turning out babies, possibly.

"Not him. Deborah."

"What?"

"Didn't you notice how big she's getting? She's gotta be about five months pregnant. Maybe six."

Lela huffed indignantly, not having noticed any such thing. "Hasn't she ever heard of birth control? My goodness! How irresponsible can the woman be? How old is she?"

"Twenty-nine, I think. She had Ronnie when she was sixteen but didn't marry his daddy until after they graduated from high school. When that didn't work out, maybe she thought Leo wanted to marry her and settle down. But he didn't."

"How is it that you know all about this woman and you live on the opposite end of the block?"

"It helps being a lunch lady at Whistler."

"They talk about such things at an elementary school?" Lela shook her head. "Anyway, when are you going to quit that job? You don't have to work, y'know."

"I love being around the kids."

"The kids who complain about the food?"

"They don't complain about my cookies." Barbara's cookies were legendary. "Anyway, I don't think Deborah and her son will have a very merry Christmas. I wanna get them a little something."

"And how is it *your* responsibility to see that they do? Honestly, Barbara, you always get involved in someone's life." *And can barely handle your own.* She almost slipped and brought up Barbara's daughter, who got pregnant, dropped out of college, married, and divorced within the space of

three years, then sustained a series of retail jobs until finally moving back home with Barbara. Alicia's baby was now in college.

Barbara fingered a rack of dresses for little girls. "Isn't this precious?" She pulled out a dress with a bright yellow sun on the front. It reminded Lela of the quilt pattern waiting for her at home.

"When is she due?"

Barbara shrugged.

"You don't even know what she's gonna have. What if she has another boy?" She suddenly thought of the quilt again. She quickly brushed the thought out of her mind.

"Why are you so negative these days, Le?" Barbara asked quietly.

Lela's head snapped up so quickly, her neck hurt. "I'm *not* negative."

"Yes, you are. You were negative when I brought up the suggestion about making the quilt. You've got a negative spirit all around these days."

"Got a lot on my mind."

Barbara's look was instantly sympathetic. She rubbed

Lela's arm. "You've had a hard year, last year. Is that it? Wanna talk about it?"

Barbara sometimes reminded her of Jean, always delving into feelings and wanting to explore them to the fullest. She suddenly felt a headache coming on. "No."

She tried to ignore Barbara's grunt and shake of the head. Suddenly she just wanted to go home.

8

*I*f she had to categorize Wednesday, she would say that it was a day that inspired a thousand sighs, starting with the ride to Bible study. Other than saying, "It was your turn to drive, if I'm not mistaken," Barbara was mostly silent as she drove Lela to Bible class. Yet her sighs seemed to speak volumes.

Lela hadn't felt the need to reply, seeing as how they were already in Barbara's car anyway. She was content to watch the familiar passing scenery.

This week, a screen had been lowered on one wall of the fellowship room—the usual signal that Lorraine or Donna planned to use PowerPoint to display a Scripture passage.

Donna moved to the podium. "Let's get started. We have a lot to cover," she cautioned, as Lela made her way through the room to her usual table.

But getting them settled took far longer than the usual fifteen-minute scramble for doughnuts and muffins, thanks to an impromptu Christmas cookie and gift exchange. As usual, Barbara's to-die-for sugar cookies (drowning in butter) and Nita's peanut blossoms ("with a hint of cinnamon") were a hit. They were considered the best cooks in the group.

"How did delving in the life of Mary go, ladies?" Donna asked when everyone had finally settled.

Nita ventured after several moments of silence, "I just realized how little I knew about Mary. She was a strong lady."

"Did any of you notice anything unusual happening this week as you were reading about Mary?"

"I seemed to have *more* problems than usual," Estelle said quietly. "My washing machine broke and I found out . . . well, I found out something about someone I wished I hadn't."

A note of sadness in Estelle's voice caused Lela to turn all the way around in her seat to look. For once she didn't seem to be dressed as if desperately seeking attention. In fact, she

seemed subdued, in a red sweatshirt and jeans, almost as if she didn't want to call attention to herself.

"That's what happens when you start delving into God's Word." Donna quickly tapped the computer on the podium to project a Scripture passage on the screen. The passage of choice was Luke 1:26–38.

"This is where it all started—the announcement that changed her life. This is one of those real-life touched-by-an-angel moments." A few of the women chuckled. "She was probably just a young teen, someone you wouldn't pay much attention to. If you were living in her day and *did* pay attention to her, you might dismiss her, thinking that she's just like all the other irresponsible, pregnant teens who can't keep their legs closed."

Lela winced at the word *irresponsible*. She'd used that descriptor for Deborah. But Deborah *was* irresponsible and a grown woman to boot—a grown woman who had access to birth control pills. And she'd gotten pregnant, obviously, when she was a teen.

"So, why do you think God chose her to have his Son, even knowing that others would definitely misunderstand her?"

"Because she was from David's tribe?" someone at a table behind Lela's volunteered. "The Messiah was prophesied to come from David's family line."

Donna gave a considering nod. "That's a good reason. Any others?"

There was silence for a few moments, before Estelle tentatively spoke up. "Because maybe he knew he could count on her to say yes?"

Lela started to roll her eyes but then found herself considering Estelle's response. She hadn't expected something so astute from Estelle.

"Sometimes God asks hard things of us. Like when he told Noah to build a boat to prepare for a rainstorm of the magnitude that had never happened before. And God was asking a woman not yet married to bear the stigma of a child many would consider illegitimate."

The "not yet married" phrase resonated with Lela. She'd always considered Mary married at this point, since an engagement in the Jewish culture was as binding as marriage. But she *wasn't* married. And she could have been stoned to death when others discovered that her husband-to-be was *not* the father of her child.

"Do you think maybe her parents were upset about what happened?" someone asked.

Donna shrugged. "The Bible doesn't reveal if her parents were alive when she heard the news. I always wondered how they would have reacted had they known about the baby. Would they have believed her? Or would they have reacted with disappointment, as some of us have when we found out our girls were pregnant or our sons got someone else's daughter pregnant?"

Lela could see a few heads nodding.

"We *do* know that Mary wasn't afraid to ask questions. After all, a pretty logical question to ask is, 'How will this be?' She wasn't being belligerent, though. She was simply curious."

Just like Jean, thought Lela. Jean had had an insatiable curiosity, always wondering why something had to be. Sometimes the girl had simply worn her out with her questions. "Why would so-and-so do such-and-such?" She simply couldn't accept "Don't worry about it" as a final answer. She always had to probe and pry. In the past, Lela thought she was simply belligerent, nosy, or stubborn, depending on the situation.

"If you noticed," Donna continued, "Mary pondered things deeply, rather than spouting an opinion without thinking through the matter first."

Just at that moment, Lela caught a look from Barbara, one that she resented. It seemed to say, *Unlike you,* as plainly as if she'd spoken the words. Was that what she was hinting at the other day with her speech about Lela's alleged negativity? Could she help it if she was plainspoken? *Somebody* had to tell the truth.

She was so busy with her thoughts that she barely noticed that Donna sat down and Lorraine stood to make a final announcement. "Don't forget we're *not* meeting next Wednesday. See you on Sunday or after Christmas. Have a blessed week, y'all."

After a closing song, the study was over. Lela collected the gifts she had received, noting those that would need regifting soon. But as she got up to follow Barbara out the door, she noticed that Estelle stayed behind.

"Estelle looks worried about something," Lela remarked.

"You noticed."

Lela huffed, making a small angry cloud on the chilly air. "Are you saying I don't notice things right under my nose, Barbara Wiggins?"

"Well, I—"

"First, I'm negative, and now I don't notice things."

"I'm keeping my mouth shut." Barbara made the zipper motion across her mouth. But she broke her vow when they arrived at her car after a two-block walk in the frosty air. "Wanna stop off for some lunch somewhere?"

"Are you sure you wanna be seen with someone so negative?"

"I'm sorry I ever said anything!"

Unlike the weather, Lela was willing to thaw and be Christian. "Someplace cheap, then." She couldn't help recalling the unexpected furnace repair bill. "I've got a taste for some chicken."

"There's the Harold's on 115th. We can take it back to your house."

Soon they were settled at Lela's dining room table with hot mugs of tea, Harold's chicken wings, and Smokey rubbing against their legs as he serenaded them with his begging yowl. "You know we don't have any business eating this."

"Yeah, but it's good. Where'd you get that print?" Barbara suddenly pointed to the Annie Lee print in the living room.

"Girl, you know Jean bought it for my birthday three years ago."

"Yeah, but where did she get it?"

"I think she bought it at a store in Glenwood." To think that Jean thought the picture reminded her of their relationship. She felt a wave of sadness suddenly. Was that how Jean saw her, as someone just to make demands of her, who seemed to spoil her fun like the mother in the print demanding that her daughter spit out her gum? Had she been that way—demanding instead of pondering like Mary?

"She's such a sweet girl."

Lela nodded. "I've always been proud of her."

"Does she know that?"

Lela's head snapped up, in time to see Barbara sneaking chicken to Smokey. "What are you suggesting?"

Barbara suddenly looked innocent. "Just asking."

"Of *course* she knows." But suddenly she wasn't so sure—not about Jean, not about Estelle, not about anyone. "What about Alicia?"

Barbara suddenly smiled; it was a fond smile Lela usually

saw on her face when Alicia was mentioned. "She knows I love her. I tell her so every day."

That's why you've got your forty-year-old daughter still living with you. She needs to grow up.

She had raised her daughters to be independent, to not need to come back home. And they didn't. Sometimes they didn't *visit* either. But they had families of their own and busy lives.

Too busy for their mama? a nagging voice at the back of her head queried.

"I think Estelle's worried about her job."

Lela had almost forgotten about Estelle. "What does she *do* anyway?"

"Administrative assistant at a law firm. They're making cutbacks on the job, like they are everywhere else."

"Don't tell me you feel the need to buy *her* something for Christmas *too*."

"You're determined to work my last nerve today, aren't you?"

"I'm keeping my mouth shut," Lela mimicked.

"Well, I'll leave you to it." Barbara saluted, as she picked up her trash and deposited it in the garbage can under the

sink. With another salute, she headed out the front door. Lela only grunted a good-bye.

With a sigh, she lit one of the cinnamon-scented candles someone had given her at Bible study, then sat on the couch to brood. She was still irked by Barbara's words and especially that look she'd given her at Bible study in response to Donna's words about Mary pondering. Okay, so maybe she did things the opposite of Mary—speaking *before* pondering. But what of it?

Lela's forthrightness usually frustrated Jean most of all in the family. Lela had always believed Jean was too sensitive for her own good.

"You need to develop a thicker skin," she'd told her over and over. *Well, she did, didn't she, in order to survive in the world? Otherwise, she'd be chewed up and spit out.* She would've failed in her job as a parent if she hadn't pointed that out.

The phone suddenly rang—a welcome interruption. "Hey, Mama." It was Sylvie's cheerful voice.

"Sylvie! It's so good to hear your voice! You just made my day."

"Glad to hear that! You just get back from Bible study?"

"Yes."

"Listen, Mama, remember that picture you sent me of the cat you found in the alley? I looked online to try to find what breed he might be. But one of my colleagues at Wesleyan solved that mystery. Smokey is a Russian blue."

"And that means what, dear?" Why was she bringing up Smokey? Sometimes Lela couldn't keep up with the way Sylvie took off on conversational tangents. She wondered if Sylvie did that while lecturing to students at Indiana Wesleyan.

"They cost a lot of money, Mama. Maybe whoever dumped him in the alley didn't know what they had. They're supposed to be really good cats."

Lela glanced at Smokey, who was currently sprawled on his back, trying to lick his chest. Not the most flattering of postures. Maybe Smokey was a sign of God's favor—unlooked for and unnoticed. She suddenly felt a wave of gratitude.

"And I was talking to Jean about Doug. Apparently, he's been acting a fool again—flaunting some woman he's with. I

think she's a nurse at the hospital where he did his residency. He was seen around town by Bud and Angela."

The wave of gratitude suddenly ebbed, replaced by the icy chill of disappointment. "How are you hearing this?"

"Rhoda told me. She heard it from Bud."

Lela bristled at the thought of Rhoda and her cousin gossiping about her granddaughter and grandson-in-law.

So much for having a doctor in the family. She'd been so proud of Doug. Now she couldn't help wondering what he'd put Darcie through to cause her to say "Enough is enough."

"Darcie could've told me this."

"Maybe she thought you'd just lecture."

"That's just what your sister said."

"You don't sound convinced."

"And why should I be? I've only ever tried to do what's best for my daughters and my grandchildren. I'm sorry if I'm perceived as so critical."

"Mama . . . see, you can't even take criticism. You just choose to see the negative side of everything."

First Jean, then Barbara, and now Sylvie? "I don't see that I—"

"Mama, I'd love to chat more, but I've got to go. I just called you quickly from my cell."

"Well, fine then. If you can't spare five minutes to talk to your critical mother—"

"I'll call you later in the week. Bean sends his love. Did you get my Christmas gifts?"

"They're under the tree."

"Well, open them!"

"Is it Christmas?"

"Mama, open the gifts!"

"I *thought* you had to go."

"Mama . . ."

"Fine." She put down the receiver, then went in search of the packages, bringing them back to the kitchen. "I'm opening the first one." She balanced the receiver against her ear as she tore off the paper to reveal a CD from a Christian artist she didn't particularly like. "Uh, thanks." It wasn't so much the gift as the thought behind it—or lack thereof. She thought Sylvie knew her better than this. "You didn't have to send anything."

The second package held an assortment of teas with names

like Sultry Cinnamon and Purple Passion that made her feel embarrassed just reading them. But she thanked Sylvie.

She knew what she was getting from Tamara—a Liz Claiborne purse or a Ferragamo gift card. Tamara was usually very generous and knew what she liked. She could have sworn that Sylvie did too.

"I need to go, Mama."

"Bye, Darcie."

"Mama, did you just call me Darcie?"

"Darcie? Why would I call you Darcie?"

"You just did."

"Guess she's always at the back of my mind these days. I wish she were coming here. I wish *you* were here." She hated the wistful note in her voice.

Sylvie either didn't hear it or chose to ignore it. "Bye, Mama."

After hanging up, Lela fished under the tree and quickly found Tamara's gift. Just as she thought. Tamara had been generous: a $300 Ferragamo gift card. But instead of the card, she suddenly wished her daughter was there.

"You sure you're up for shoe shopping today?" asked Barbara soon after she and Alicia pulled up in front of the house.

"Gotta spend this gift card. Didn't know you were coming," Lela added to Alicia. She certainly hadn't suggested including Alicia when she called Barbara the previous day.

Alicia was a younger, more freckled version of her mother. They had the same round build, the same inviting grin. Alicia usually kept her short hair in a permed bob. Evidently she was proud of it, having chosen to forgo wearing a hat in the frigid weather.

"She volunteered to drive and on her day off too," said Barbara, with a fond look at her daughter.

Alicia grinned. "I couldn't leave you two old ladies to run the streets alone. You couldn't find your way to Aurora without me. At least it's not supposed to snow today."

Barbara quickly vacated the front seat, indicating with a wave of her hand that Lela was to take her place. Lela climbed in the front seat of Alicia's Escalade with a grunt.

As they headed north on the Dan Ryan, Alicia asked, "You sure you don't wanna head up to Gurnee Mills?"

"That's a longer drive, isn't it?" As far as Lela was concerned, that was the end of it.

Alicia shrugged. "Got nothing but time today."

"Put on some music," said Barbara.

"Old lady music or something good? . . . Ow!"

Lela could almost feel the pinch Barbara gave her daughter.

Alicia laughed as she switched on WMBI. "This is your station, Mama."

"It Came Upon a Midnight Clear" soon made its presence known.

Within an hour and a half, thanks to an accident that slowed traffic to a crawl on the Eisenhower, they were pulling up in the parking lot at the outlet mall. Lela grumbled at the distance they had to walk, thanks to an abundance of Christmas shoppers. She almost regretted the trip.

Soon they were in the small shop, which boasted shoes and purses reeking of expense. Ignoring the offers of assistance from the persistent saleswomen, Lela took her time looking over the merchandise.

"I like these pumps." Barbara picked up a gray one with a hole at the toes.

"Five-inch heels." Lela looked askance at the shoe.

"I didn't say I'd *wear* them. I just said I like these pumps. You know there was a time when we used to wear stuff like this."

"A hundred years and another lifetime ago."

Barbara tapped her sensible flat heel against the floor. "I leave that to the younger generation."

"Even *I* don't wear those," Alicia quipped.

"What about those black shoes of yours?"

"Mama, the heels are only this big." Alicia brought her thumb and index finger about two inches apart. "Maybe you need to sit down and get some blood circulating in that head of yours."

Barbara flopped onto a chair. "Yes'm."

Lela envied Barbara's easy camaraderie with Alicia. They always joked around like that. She couldn't remember the last time she laughed with Tamara or Sylvie. Certainly not with Jean.

Lela fingered a pair of white flats with a fuchsia satin buckle. Nearly $400 on sale. Out of her price range. Normally, the thought of being able to spend $300 on

whatever—an extravagance—excited her. But suddenly, she felt depressed.

Walt used to joke that when a woman went shoe shopping, she was either troubled about something or about to cause trouble. She'd always brushed his remark aside. But not today.

"Have you decided what you want?" one the saleswomen asked, interrupting her reverie. Lela selected the first pair of shoes that fit, barely blinking at the $250 price tag. Her heart was no longer in the shopping; she simply wanted to keep the trip from being a complete waste of time.

By the time she arrived home that evening, she was physically exhausted and missing Walt like crazy.

She barely noticed Smokey looking for his dinner, barely noticed that she was hungry herself and missing *Wheel of Fortune*. Suddenly her mind flashed back to that evening in 1975 when Walt got so angry with her buying a pair of shoes. It was only after they'd had a screaming battle that she realized he'd been laid off from his job and they couldn't afford the money she spent.

Finally, Smokey's yowling pierced through the gloom. She

fed him and fed herself some leftover ham from Frank's. But she barely tasted anything.

She flipped on the lights and took out her piecework. But then she thought, *I should just go to bed.* After a quick shower, she did just that, too tired to fight any longer. She didn't even mind when Smokey flopped his little bold self onto the pillow next to hers again.

9

At eight thirty on Friday morning she left a message for Tamara to call the Social Security office and remind them that she wasn't dead. Perhaps if they heard from someone else, they would be more inclined to speed things along. In the meantime, there was Mary's life to ponder over in a blissfully warm house that Lela's $450 investment had provided. Oddly enough, though, the weather was now nice, sunny, and 45 degrees. Oh well. At least the sun helped lift the previous day's gloom.

This time, she turned to Luke 2 to hear the story of Jesus' birth—the fourth passage on the Scripture list.

LUKE 2:1–8

And it came to pass in those days, that there went out a decree from Caesar Augustus that all the world should

be taxed. (And this taxing was first made when Cyrenius was governor of Syria.) And all went to be taxed, every one into his own city. And Joseph also went up from Galilee, out of the city of Nazareth, into Judea, unto the city of David, which is called Bethlehem (because he was of the house and lineage of David), to be taxed with Mary his espoused wife, being great with child. And so it was, that, while they were there, the days were accomplished that she should be delivered. And she brought forth her firstborn son, and wrapped him in swaddling clothes, and laid him in a manger; because there was no room for them in the inn. And there were in the same country shepherds abiding in the field, keeping watch over their flock by night.

She soon felt lulled by the powerful voice of the actor who read the story of Mary having her baby. She sighed as she picked up the quilt pattern, absently noting that the fourth block called for a smiling sun.

She could hardly imagine the indignity of bearing a child in a filthy stable. It was hard enough having a "Negro" child born in an underfunded hospital in Mississippi back in 1961,

as her firstborn, Tamara, had been. Yet the soon-to-be savior of the world—the God of the universe—had been born in utter squalor surrounded by animals, all because there was no room for him in the inn.

"Is there room for him in *your* heart?" asked the pastor in his sermon last year at Christmas. *Of course there is, Lord,* she had thought. *There's always room for Your Son.* But now she suddenly wondered if the Holy Spirit brought the question to mind because he meant God's son or someone else.

She turned the CD back to the beginning of Luke 2 and listened to the story again.

"She gave birth to her firstborn, a son," read the actor.

Was Mary's labor long? Stubborn Tamara had put her through twenty hours of labor before she finally came, squalling, little hands clenched and arms flailing, showing plenty of attitude that she still hadn't lost, even after forty-eight years.

Tam had been first in everything. First in her class in high school. Graduated magna cum laude from Howard University. Made law review at Princeton.

Sylvie, who was born in 1967, had been two weeks early, while Jean had come just when the doctor said she would. No surprises there. Sylvie was her "smiling sun"—a happy

baby who blossomed into a happy child and finally a happy, laid-back adult. Jean had been a happy baby too, come to think of it. It was only later when she reached the tumultuous teen years that she seemed to complain about her sisters getting the attention she felt she was denied. And now she seemed to feel that Darcie needed to be protected from her own grandmama!

Jean.

Darcie.

Why hadn't she heard from Darcie or Jean? She tried Jean's number. Busy. Surely Darcie was there by now.

Finally, Jean picked up the phone when Lela called again just after seven that evening. "You just missed Darcie. She's out Christmas shopping with her sister. Jas is finally home from college."

Lela didn't want to talk about her other granddaughter just then. "Why is the girl always out when I call? Am I supposed to think she's avoiding me?"

"Mother, I told you she's vulnerable right now."

"When she was a little girl, Darcie used to call *me* when she had a fight with *you*."

"I think she's afraid you'll go off on her."

"I wouldn't—"

"Let's face it, Mother, you *would*. There's no secret about how you feel about divorce. Remember when Cousin Ruth and Tucker divorced two years ago?"

Everyone knew how wild Oby's daughter, Ruth, was, which was why she wound up leaving Tucker for the next man to catch her fancy. Lela never approved of how Obadiah raised that girl. She hadn't bothered making the child a quilt, because she'd had a feeling Ruth's marriage wouldn't last.

The thought brought her up short. She hadn't made *Darcie* a quilt either. Had she the same feeling? But no. It couldn't be. She had simply been reeling from Mama's death. There had hardly been any time to grieve with Darcie getting married a month later. Not that any of them were really surprised. Mama had been poorly the last couple of years. Previously she'd been relatively robust in health; it seemed like the cancer that took her had been waiting to catch up with her the last five years, like an assassin, finally reaching its mark.

"Mother? Are you there?"

She suddenly realized she hadn't answered Jean's question. She paused before saying, "Darcie could've called me. She knows she can always talk to me."

Jean sighed. "Mother, you *never* think about what somebody else is going through."

"*I* never think? What do you think I've *been* thinking about ever since you told me?"

Lela had a sudden, horrible thought. Maybe she *had* known deep down that Darcie and Doug's marriage wouldn't last either. She had sometimes caught Doug looking at Darcie, when he didn't know he was being observed those last few months before the wedding, when the last-minute changes drove everyone crazy. He had looked trapped, like a man who wanted to know where the exits were. But at the time, she believed it was just nerves.

"I meant you're not thinking about how Darcie might be feeling right now. You don't listen sometimes."

"Jean, I told you all that listening to her feelings wouldn't help her. Now she's feeling herself out of a marriage she probably could have worked out."

"So, now this is *my* fault? Doug cheats on her, and it's *my* fault?"

"I didn't say it was—"

But Jean had hung up.

She called back half an hour later. "Mother—"

"Why didn't you ever call me Mama like your sisters?" The words suddenly burst out of her mouth, more than thirty-three years in the making.

"Huh?"

"You haven't called me Mama since you were fourteen. It's like you're keeping me at a distance."

Jean was silent for a bit. "I always thought Mother was elegant. Like you."

Lela suddenly felt pierced to the soul and exasperated at the same time. Elegant? What exactly did that mean? It sounded like a backward sort of compliment that didn't add up to "I love you" or, and she hated thinking this, "You're my favorite."

"And maybe I did, really," Jean continued. "Hold you at a distance that is. I didn't always feel comfortable around you. I could tell Daddy some things I couldn't tell you."

She'd heard this song before. Of course Walt had the time to listen. She had all the housework to do on top of teaching third grade. That's why Walt always had time to play with the girls even after teaching at the high school all day.

"I know you adored him. He had time to play. I had to get you ready for school, get your homework done, and get myself to work day after day."

"Mama—" Jean's voice suddenly broke. "This isn't a contest between you and Daddy. You know I love you, don't you? Why don't you understand that?"

But Lela was too hurt to hear. "Tell Darcie when she wants to call, she knows where I am. Gotta go." This time, she was the one to hang up without saying good-bye.

10

The conversation with Jean felt like an oil slick on her soul all day Saturday. All the while she went about her household tasks, she thought about calling and apologizing.

When was the last time she said "I'm sorry" to Jean or Tam or Sylvie, she wondered. Her heart plunged even further when she couldn't remember a time. She'd always subscribed to the I'm-your-mama-and-therefore-right school of thought. That was how it was with Marie Johnson Williams, *her* mama.

She suddenly remembered a smile on Mama's face during a visit to the large farmhouse Mama still occupied in Mississippi when Jean was seven, back in 1970. Something must have happened between Mama and Jean, because just

before Lela entered the large kitchen, she heard Mama's soft voice saying, "Oh, baby, Grandmama's sorry."

There was a pause before Jean said, "That's okay." She soon began chattering about something else, already acting on the full forgiveness "That's okay" implied.

Yet Mama's apology caused her to rock back on her heels. Had Mama *ever* apologized to *her* or to her brothers? Lela couldn't recall a time. But when the grandchildren had come, Mama had been different than she was when Lela and her brothers were growing up. And Mama had always been more patient with Jean, as if they had a special bond.

It was easy for Jean to get along with Mama, seeing as how Mama seemed to always have time for her. Mama babied Jean too much, giving her treats even though Lela told her the girls didn't need the sugar. Mama hadn't had much time to baby Lela, not with a bunch of sons (and Lela) getting into things. Mama was old-school anyway. She had Lela cooking and washing at the age of nine and later taking care of her younger brothers.

Lela mentally shook herself. *I need to take my mind off this.* She filled the teakettle and set it on the stove. Waiting

for the water to boil, she gazed at the sheet given to her at Bible study. Lorraine and Donna had listed nine passages of Scripture for the group to read. She'd left the quilt pattern on the table. There were nine blocks on the quilt top.

Luke 2:8–21

And there were in the same country shepherds abiding in the field, keeping watch over their flock by night. And, lo, the angel of the Lord came upon them, and the glory of the Lord shone round about them: and they were sore afraid. And the angel said unto them, Fear not: for, behold, I bring you good tidings of great joy, which shall be to all people. For unto you is born this day in the city of David a Saviour, which is Christ the Lord. And this shall be a sign unto you; Ye shall find the babe wrapped in swaddling clothes, lying in a manger. And suddenly there was with the angel a multitude of the heavenly host praising God, and saying, Glory to God in the highest, and on earth peace, good will toward men. And it came to pass, as the angels were gone away from them into heaven, the shepherds said one to another, Let us now go even unto

Bethlehem, and see this thing which is come to pass, which the Lord hath made known unto us. And they came with haste, and found Mary and Joseph, and the babe lying in a manger. And when they had seen it, they made known abroad the saying which was told them concerning this child. And all they that heard it wondered at those things which were told them by the shepherds. But Mary kept all these things, and pondered them in her heart. And the shepherds returned, glorifying and praising God for all the things that they had heard and seen, as it was told unto them. And when eight days were accomplished for the circumcising of the child, his name was called JESUS, which was so named of the angel before he was conceived in the womb.

The fifth Scripture passage to be read was Luke 2:8–21—the shepherds' glimpse of the newborn Savior. She eyed the fifth block in the quilt pattern with an awe she hadn't felt before. The pattern called for a cat. And the story was about shepherds leaving their sheep to catch a glimpse of the Savior. A cat wasn't a sheep, but a cat was an *animal*. And the beach

ball in the first block? While it didn't overtly remind her of an element of Mary's journey, isn't that where God got the ball rolling in the first place with the announcement of Jesus' birth? And what about the second block—a baby's foot? It now reminded her of John the Baptist in his mother's womb jumping for joy. And the third—the heart—well, that had marriage written all over it, didn't it?

She waited a few minutes before switching on the CD, trying to let it all sink in. She suddenly felt pushed, like a log swirling along the rapids of a river. This was God's doing, obviously. But why, why?

With no answer forthcoming, she switched on the CD and listened with a desperate eagerness. She tried to imagine what it must have been like for Mary seeing the shepherds running in, grubby and desperate for a glimpse of her baby. What must Mary have thought when they trooped in, probably smelling of sheep? Did she start forward anxiously as the tiny Savior was lifted over and over by calloused hands and passed around? Their eagerness probably gave her plenty of food for thought.

Lela recalled her own eagerness to show pictures of each

of her daughters, especially at Christmastime. Nowadays everything was instant this or that, thanks to digital cameras. But when Tamara was a baby, relatives far away had to wait until film was developed to see her.

Smokey suddenly leaped into her lap, as if realizing that the story Lela read concerned animals. Or perhaps he was interested in the cat for the fifth block that she traced on tan fabric. She pushed him aside with her elbow.

Restlessness wafted over her, like a breeze she couldn't ignore. She suddenly desperately wanted to get out of the house. But there was nowhere she needed to go.

Smokey suddenly curled around her feet, his little body warm against her socked toes. It was almost as if he sensed her restlessness and wanted to keep her at home with him.

When the phone rang a minute later, she knew it would be Jean. Knew it and was fiercely grateful that it was.

"I hate it when we fight, Mother." Jean's voice sounded small, as if she were a child again.

Lela felt a lump in her throat. "How are things there?" That was as close to "sorry" as she was going to get.

Jean didn't say anything for a few moments. When her voice came, it sounded resigned. "Okay. Everyone sends their love."

Then why don't I get to talk to everyone?

"Wanna speak to Darcie? I think she's ready to talk now."

Lela's anger flared. "Are you her therapist now?"

"Mother, I'm just trying to pick up the pieces here. I know you never approved of what I do."

"I never said I didn't."

"I *like* what I do, Mother."

"Then why didn't you finish your doctorate? You could have gone farther. I wanted you to have everything I didn't have, go farther than I could go."

"Go where, Mother? To a place I don't really have to be? I like where I am. I see clients when I want to."

"Yes, but isn't your friend Rita a psychiatrist?"

Jean sighed. "Are you *still* upset that I didn't go to medical school? Is that what this about?"

Before Lela could respond, Jean continued. "Aren't you reading about Mary?"

"How'd you find that out?"

"Mrs. Wiggins. Seems to me the only thing God asked *her* to do was to have his child. I wanted to work as a therapist and raise my kids. I did what I believed God wanted me to do. You were a teacher. Did you want to be something else?"

She'd thought about being a school principal at one point. But that would have meant going back to school to get a master's degree. She'd had her hands full just finishing her undergraduate degree and getting certified as a teacher after Tamara came into the world.

"Did you want to talk to Darcie? I can put her on."

Suddenly, she didn't know what to say to Darcie. And she certainly didn't feel like fighting with anyone else.

"Or Jasmine's here," Jean suddenly added. "Want to speak to her?"

Right now, talking to Jasmine seemed safer. "Put her on."

Even soon after she hung up, she couldn't remember much about the exchange with Jasmine. The girl usually talked fast and rattled off names of friends and subjects that Lela couldn't exactly recall. Still, it was wonderful to hear her voice.

Lela moved to the front window, watching the lights blink

on and off at the neighbors' Vegas-like house across the street. In comparison, her only decoration was a wreath with blinking lights on the door. She counted on either Darcie putting up the lights or getting one of the neighbor kids to put lights on the bushes.

So why wasn't the wreath blinking? Did someone steal one of her bulbs again? She marched out to the porch, momentarily forgetting that she still wore her monkey slippers, as she inspected the effect from outside.

She turned at the sound of a car suddenly passing and saw a newer model Volkswagen Beetle cruise to the curb in front of Deborah's house. There came a sound like a car backfiring and glass breaking, then the car slipped around the corner.

With the shock of it and the ridiculousness of a gunshot coming from a Volkswagen Beetle, she suddenly found herself slipping down the five stairs of her porch. She scrabbled madly for the porch rail, her left ankle slamming against the last step.

The next thing she knew, Deborah was running over from across the street while James hurried over from next door.

"Were ya sho—?" James began.

"I saw you fall! Are you okay?" Deborah interrupted, clutching at Lela's left arm, as if to lift her from her supine position against the stairs.

Lela slowly released the porch rail as she eased herself into a seated position. "Of course I'm not okay!" She felt bruised all over, immensely cranky, and foolish, like a cliché of the elderly.

"You need to go to the hospital?"

"Thought I heard a shot," James insisted. "Thought maybe it was you when you fell. Somebody needs to call the *po*lice."

"I just called nine-one-one. They're sending the police," Deborah said.

"They need to send an ambu—"

"I don't *need* to go to the hospital. I just need to sit here for a moment and catch my breath." Lela tried to ignore the throbbing in her left ankle. Both palms felt scraped.

"Don't you want a doctor to check you? You might have broken a hip."

"Oh, that can be dangerous," said James.

"My *hip* is not the problem!" She rubbed her left ankle.

"It probably needs some ice or something. Put some snow

on it." Deborah scooped up some snow with her bare hands from the grass and plopped it on Lela's foot.

"What are you doing?!"

"It might be broken. If so, you're supposed to put ice on it. I read that on the Internet."

Lela didn't care what Deborah read at that moment. She just wanted both of them to go away and stop chattering at her.

James seemed to take the hint and returned home. But why was Deborah being so helpful now of all times, when somebody had taken a shot at her house?

"Lemme get you a blanket or something."

Lela didn't want Deborah running around in her house. "That's not neces—"

But Deborah ran in the house, soon returning with a red throw from the couch. "Here. This'll keep you warm."

Lela grunted her thanks. There was something else to be grateful for at least: she wore the charcoal gray fleece warm-up suit Tamara had given her on her birthday, as well as a pair of Walter's old socks.

"Want me to call Barbara and see if she's home?" Deborah

took out a cell phone and dialed it before Lela could respond.

Lela felt guilty. Sidney was in town finally, and Barbara and her family were probably having a meal. And she couldn't get over the fact that Deborah was being so helpful, even in the midst of her own problems. *She'd* never offered to help Deborah.

Within ten minutes, Barbara pulled up in front of the house and hurried out of the car. "Girl, are you okay? How do you feel? And why is your foot covered in snow? It's thirty degrees out here!"

"I think she landed on her foot wr—"

"I feel cold, stupid, and in pain," Lela interrupted Deborah. "I couldn't make it back up the stairs. Help me up. I just need to sit on the couch for a minute."

"You *need* to go to the hospital."

"Quit fussing." The throbbing in her ankle seemed to prove Barbara right. She needed to go to the hospital.

"I'll go in and find you some shoes and get your coat."

"Find my purse too!"

Twenty minutes later, just as Lela hobbled toward Barbara's car wearing one tennis shoe and one bedroom slipper with

a cheerful monkey face over a steadily swelling foot, three police cruisers squealed up, along with an ambulance, which pulled up alongside Barbara's car.

One of the paramedics hurried to her side, while the other pulled a stretcher out of the back of the ambulance.

"One of you call for an ambulance?" the paramedic asked. With his unlined, clean-shaven face, he barely looked older than Deborah's son, Ronnie.

"I *didn't* call for one. I don't *need* one. She'll drive me," said Lela, nodding to Barbara.

"But we were told that someone had been shot," said the stretcher bearer, who had joined his partner. "Here, why don't you sit down at least?"

"What's the trouble?" asked his partner.

Lela felt immensely foolish as the paramedics helped her onto the stretcher. "I fell down the stairs."

"Are you feeling disoriented?" the first paramedic asked in a slow, measured voice. "What is your name?"

Before she could give him the sarcastic answer on the tip of her tongue, two police officers joined the ring of people surrounding her. One was female and had an olive complexion

that indicated an ethnicity of some sort. Lela couldn't quite tell which ethnicity in the dim light. Both, however, had the been-there-done-that look of those who had seen the same scene over and over again.

"What happened here?" asked the female officer.

"A drive-by!" James yelled from his porch. "Gangs have been breaking into garages around here!"

"Is this the gunshot victim?" the other officer asked the paramedics, with a nod toward Lela.

"No."

Lela resented someone else being asked a question about her health. *"I wasn't shot!"*

"It wasn't like that," Deborah said quietly—so quietly that Lela almost wasn't sure she heard. "Somebody shot at my front window. It's all busted out."

Lela couldn't see whether or not it was from that distance.

Both officers turned to Lela. "Were you outside when it happened?" asked the female.

"I was on my *own* porch minding my *own* business!" Lela snapped.

"You should never come out of your house during a shoot-

ing," the other officer chided. "You could've been seriously injured."

"I didn't come out because of *that*!"

The two officers exchanged a look, one Lela didn't want to interpret.

"My window's busted," Deborah reminded them.

The male officer gave a crisp nod. "Let's take a look."

Deborah returned to her house, escorted by the two officers. But two more police officers soon drifted over. One had a flashlight, which he aimed at the houses.

By then, curious neighbors had begun spilling out of their houses. Lela grunted as she spotted the couple who lived in the house at the left of hers heading toward her. Both had on exercise apparel, as if they had just returned from the health club.

"Let's get this area cleared," one of the officers said. "Unless you have pertinent information, please go back to your homes while we look around."

"We were both home when we heard a shot," said the husband. "We only came out when we thought it was safe."

"A wise move, sir," said the officer, as he moved toward Lela's backyard. The other officer followed.

"Can we go? My foot's cold!" Lela snapped to Barbara.

"Are you sure you don't wanna ride in the ambulance?" asked Barbara. "They'll get you there faster."

"I'm sure I don't, Barbara Wiggins, unless for some reason you'd prefer not to drive me to the hospital!"

Both paramedics wheeled her to the waiting car and helped her to sit on the front seat.

"They were really helpful," said Barbara, as she pulled away.

"Stop the car!" Lela shouted, just as Barbara approached the corner of 117th.

The car slid slightly at the suddenness with which Barbara slammed on her brakes. "I almost hit that police car!" she chided.

"I just thought of something. Can you have Alicia come down and watch the house? Everybody knows I'm going to the hospital. Perfect time to try to rob my house," Lela reasoned.

"With all these cops around?" Nevertheless, Barbara turned left at the corner and soon headed south on the next block. She pulled up along the curb in front of her house,

then headed inside. About ten minutes later, she returned with Alicia, who carried with her a small tin. "Some provisions for the journey," she said, trading it for Lela's house keys.

"Brownies," Barbara explained, once they dropped Alicia at the house and were headed north once more.

"Where are you taking me?"

"Roseland Hospital."

"I'd rather go out to Our Lady of Peace Hospital, if it's all the same to you."

"Sure you don't wanna go to Roseland? It's closer."

"You got somewhere to be?"

Barbara shook her head. "Sometimes I think you purposely plan to interrupt my life. Sidney says hi, by the way."

"Shanaynay with him?"

"*Shawna* is with her parents. You know they trade off sometimes. I told you about calling the girl that. I might slip up and call her that sometimes."

"Well, she looks like that comedian who used to dress up as a woman." Sidney and Shawna's lives seemed a little too separate for a married couple. She briefly thought of Doug.

"Deborah was really helpful, wasn't she?"

Lela didn't feel like talking about Deborah just then. "Turn up the heat."

"It's up."

Maybe it was the shock of the incident, but suddenly she couldn't stop shivering. She was still shivering when they arrived.

"Need a wheelchair?" a security guard asked, as soon as Barbara opened the car door.

Lela felt foolish being wheeled into the emergency wing of Our Lady of Peace Hospital on Ninety-fifth Street, still in one bedroom slipper, especially as the nurses seemed content at first to talk to Barbara about her alleged condition, as if she'd gone funny in the head.

After she was registered, the triage nurse wheeled her into room number 5 in the emergency wing. Soon a barrage of questions came her way from a chipper, heavyset nurse, who seemed to speak loudly as if Lela were deaf. Was she on Medicare? Yes. Did her chest hurt? No. Did she have a history of stroke or heart disease? Not personally. And no, she didn't know what either felt like, even though her daddy died of a stroke, and what difference did that make right now,

since it was her *foot* that hurt? She *hadn't* taken any medication that caused a severe allergic reaction. And no, she hadn't felt light-headed. Did she hit her head during the fall? No. Did her chest hurt? No, once again. (She wondered why they kept asking that question.) Her foot hurt as well as her palms where she'd gripped the icy railing for dear life. She could have kicked herself for not putting more salt on the porch.

"Your neighbor said you were outside in your slippers," said the nurse, nodding to Barbara. "Were you feeling confused or overcome and in need of some air?"

"I can't stand outside my own house? I just went out to look at the wreath on my door and slipped down the stairs."

The nurse wrote her answers on the sheet housed in the folder she carried. Lela wondered if her sanity was somehow on trial.

The nurse handed her a thin cotton gown. "Strip to the waist, please."

"I'll wait outside." Barbara patted her shoulder.

Lela tried to pull the fleece top over her head, but she soon felt the slow fire of pain in her right shoulder. She sighed heavily.

"Let me give you a hand," said the nurse.

Lela suffered through being gowned and helped back aboard the bed, with her foot propped up.

"The doctor will see you presently."

"Presently" turned out to be an hour later, when the curtain to emergency room 5 was thrown back to reveal a red-haired man around forty with dark eyes, a badge that read "Forsyth," and an affable expression on his face. The doctor, Lela presumed. She was thankful he didn't greet her with the standard, "And how are we today?" Instead he said, "Lemme guess: snowboarding?"

At least Barbara found that amusing. Lela didn't feel like cracking a smile.

She had to explain all over again what happened, while the doctor gingerly examined her foot. She winced several times and glared at him.

"We'll need to get that X-rayed. But let me take a look at those hands." He turned them over and over. "Minor abrasions. We'll get those bandaged up."

She glanced at her hands. She had a cut on each palm—cuts she barely remembered getting.

Both feet were X-rayed ("Just to be on the safe side," the

doctor had said), her throat was checked, her heart rate monitored, and blood drawn. At least they didn't ask for a stool sample, she mused with a tired shake of the head. And over and over she was asked to tell her age. She wondered if they were afraid she'd suddenly change the answer. She wanted so much to say, "I'm not senile," and above all, to prove it.

She returned to the room where she had first been taken, just as Dr. Forsyth arrived.

"You are *very* lucky," he declared, with a wide smile.

She questioned his definition of luck. Not that she believed in luck. But if she had, falling down the stairs and breaking an ankle didn't seem like her idea of "lucky." "Lucky" was winning the lottery. "Lucky" was not falling down icy stairs after hearing a gunshot.

"Your ankle is broken, yes, but not badly—just a hairline fracture. So you won't need surgery. I think your friend here said your neighbor suggested putting snow on it. You have a quick-thinking neighbor."

Lela thought of Deborah and the snow and grunted.

"We'll keep icing it to keep the swelling down. But it might swell up more overnight. If so, we won't be able to cast

it until the swelling goes down. When you get the cast, you'll still need to keep that foot elevated."

"I can go home, then?" She noted that Barbara, who had been dozing off in the corner, suddenly perked up.

"We'd like to keep you overnight for observation."

"Why?"

"Well, because of your age primarily. You were outside in the cold, weren't you?"

"Yes, but only for a short while! A half hour at most."

"A half hour in thirty-degree weather. And you seem a little dehydrated. We just want to make sure you're okay. I'm sure your family would want that. Also, you might check with your doctor about adjusting your blood pressure meds." He checked the folder on his lap. "Pressure's a bit high. I'm going to start you on an IV with some saline along with something for the pain. We'll also give your doctor a courtesy call to update her."

An hour later, after saying good-bye to Barbara, she was wheeled to one of the observation rooms—a narrow, cream-walled room just large enough for a bed, a monitor for vitals, and a wafer-slim bedside table that immediately got in the way of the IV pole in the corner.

Lela climbed onto the bed with the help of a nurse, feeling the gown flop open in the back. It had already come undone while she was being wheeled from the X-ray room back to her temporary home in the emergency wing. She felt just as equally undone with all that had happened.

What time is it? It felt very late.

After propping up Lela's foot, the nurse pointed out the controls for the bed and the intercom button. "You probably just want to get some sleep, huh?" she asked, flicking off the light before Lela answered.

Lela could not have managed an answer, had the nurse waited to hear one. As soon as the door closed softly behind the nurse, the tears flowed. She wasn't normally much of a crier. But never had she felt so out of control—so helpless and old. Would she go downhill like a friend who broke a hip and was now in the convalescent home?

Lord, please help me.

Although she didn't think she would sleep at all, she found herself waking up an unknown amount of time later. There were no visual cues as to time, the room being windowless.

Her foot was sore. The skin felt even more tightly stretched than it had hours earlier, when the nurse checked it. She fumbled for the IV controller, hoping the bag still retained some pain medication.

Someone pushed open the door to her room. Lela could only assume the blurry figure coming toward her was a nurse. "Ready to go home, Mrs. Edwards?" she asked, with more cheer than Lela currently felt.

"What time is it?" she croaked, wondering where her glasses were. She could have sworn she had them on her face when she fell asleep.

The nurse glanced at her arm. "Ten sixteen."

She never slept to this hour, especially on . . . was today Sunday? If she had to usher today, she would already be at church for the early service.

The nurse clucked over Lela's foot. "Still too swollen. Looks like you'll have to wait until tomorrow for a cast. But the doctor has signed your release. He's giving you a prescription for some pain meds."

Lela nodded, then grimaced as the nurse unhooked the IV from her hand before handing her several pieces of paper.

"Here is your discharge information and your prescription."

"My glasses?"

"In your purse." The nurse indicated the small, dark blob on the lozenge-shaped table.

Don't let the door hit you on the way out were the words that came to her mind as the nurse bustled out of the door.

Well, that was that.

Barbara arrived at eleven thirty, bringing with her condolences from "everyone" at church. Lela only half listened to the litany of messages.

"So, you're coming to my house, right?"

"You've got a house full of people already."

"Just Sidney and my grandbabies. At least stay the night so I can keep an eye on you."

Lela didn't want to argue, didn't want to talk, really. She just wanted to be alone with her thoughts.

Barbara's big, affable son Sidney met them at the garage, pushing a wheelchair—one that once was used by Barbara's husband—which drew a frown from Lela. Sidney hauled her out of the car at his mother's command.

"We're going out to eat," Barbara announced, as soon as Lela was settled in one corner of the sectional with a pillow under her foot. "You'll probably wanna rest a bit, huh? I'll make you a ham sandwich and put it right here on the coffee table."

Stop hovering, was on the tip of Lela's tongue. But she didn't say anything, favoring a nod instead.

"You'd better call Jean. She's called a few times."

Lela waited until the house was completely empty before dialing Jean's number on her cell phone. *Gotta get used to using this.*

Jean answered on the first ring. "Mother, I'm sending you a ticket, okay? I want you to come here for Christmas." Jean's voice was firm.

"Are you asking me *now* because I fell down the stairs?" She hated pity invitations. It was bad enough that she let Barbara talk her into staying down at her house for one night. At least Alicia remained at her house, watching it.

"Mother . . ." There was infinite sadness in Jean's voice, a sadness that pierced Lela. "I want to take care of you."

"Jean, I *couldn't* travel now. I don't even have a cast. Barbara'll take me on Tuesday to get one if the swelling goes down enough. Even then, I don't feel up to traveling."

"You're right, you're right. I'm just so worried about you. When I heard about what happened . . . You're going to Uncle Frank's at least, right, to spend a few days out there?"

"I'm not an invalid! Why is everyone acting like I've died or something?"

"Mother . . . would you just admit that you need help?"

She didn't feel like arguing with Jean again, not after the ugliness of their last conversation. Besides, Jean was right. "I—I'll think about going out to Frank's, okay?"

"Okay. Okay."

She barely hung up from talking to Jean when the barrage of calls began. Barnabas, Oby, Samuel, and Frank followed

in quick succession. How they heard about the matter, she could only attribute to Jean.

"You can't let someone know you're in the hospital?" Frank asked, the moment Lela answered the phone. "Oh, Sam asked me to tell you hello and that he's praying for you. He'll call you later."

"How'd you find out?"

"Jean called me. I can pick you up this afternoon and bring you out here."

"You've got a house full of people, Frank!"

"Sis, you need someone to look after you."

"Why do you think I'm here at Barbara's? Besides, I don't feel up to the long drive just now, Frank."

"Want me to send Catherine out to stay with you for a few days? I'm sure she can be apart from Vaughn that long."

"I can come out there," she heard Catherine say in the background.

"I'll think about it."

She was faintly surprised and a little depressed as the day went on and finally ended and neither Sylvie nor Tamara had called. *Maybe they're both busy.* But was that any excuse?

She awoke to the blare of sirens. A lot of sirens.

She peered at the darkened room. *What day is this? Sunday still? Monday? What time is it? And where's Smokey?*

It took almost a full minute to get her bearings. She was in Barbara's house. It was still the middle of the night. Smokey was still in *her* house with Alicia.

And then Barbara's phone began to ring and ring.

Is she going to get that?

Moments later, Lela heard could hear Barbara's voice from upstairs. "Oh, hi, Alicia. What was that now? . . . Of course, she's here. . . . *What? What* did you just say? The police? Coming down here? What for? . . . Oh, Lord God, please help us all. . . . Are you okay? . . . Okay. . . . I see. . . . Thanks for calling."

Moments later, Lela heard footsteps on the stairs.

"Good," said Barbara. "You're awake."

Lela fished around on the coffee table for her glasses. Her heart thudded at the look on Barbara's face. "What's going on? Something happened to Alicia?"

"You'd better sit down."

"I *am* sitting. What else can I do *but* sit with a broken ankle?"

"There's been . . . a shooting. . . . Someone's dead, Lela." Barbara's voice suddenly sounded heavy with tears.

"Who?" Lela's heart thudded again. She had a million scenarios in her mind, all starring someone in her family.

"It's Ronnie."

"Ronnie?" She almost thought she hadn't heard correctly.

"He was found dead. Shot to death. Outside your garage."

12

The next time she woke up, 10:00 AM stared her in the face, along with Alicia's Pekingese. Sometime during the early morning hours Libby had crawled under the blanket and was currently nestled against her neck, snoring slightly. Yet her eyes were open.

Lela shuddered. She missed Smokey.

Barbara chuckled slightly as she padded around in fuchsia slippers and a matching fuchsia and black robe. A black bandanna with white polka dots adorned her head. "Didn't think there'd be anything to laugh at today."

"Come get this dog off me."

"You didn't break your hands. Want some breakfast? There's still some ham left. I can make you some grits."

All she wanted was a cup of tea—any kind of tea that

didn't have an embarrassing name or a bayberry scent. She yawned, her back suddenly aching, and sat up, dislodging Libby. Now her right shoulder ached.

The events of the night returned forcibly to her mind, especially the two AM hourlong talk with the police. The idea of the boy being killed at or dumped by her garage still weighed heavily on her mind. She hadn't wanted to know what kind of gun was used or where Ronnie had been shot. The fact of the matter was he'd been killed. And that was horrible enough.

And she'd been unprepared when the police asked her if Ronnie was likable. What kind of question was that? She barely knew him.

"So, he was trying to get in my garage again?" she had asked them. Was theft his last act? She shook her head. What a sad waste of a young life.

She voiced the same question now to Barbara.

Barbara paused in the middle of making coffee. "You don't know that he *ever* tried. Didn't the police say his prints *weren't* found on the door anywhere?"

Lela suddenly felt petty and heartily ashamed of her

thoughts about Ronnie. "You're right. And I'm . . . I'm sorry that happened."

Barbara sank onto the couch, carefully avoiding Lela's foot. "Deborah must be going out of her mind."

"Do you think it was the same person who shot at her window?"

"She thinks it was Leo or his new girlfriend. But would they be that stupid?"

"Why do you think Leo shot the boy?"

"*If* he shot him, maybe out of spite to punish Deborah for kicking his behind out. Police are still looking for him. Coulda been a gang shooting, though. They try to recruit young boys. And I think they're the ones who've been breaking into garages." Barbara sighed. "I can just see the newspapers now, if the story even makes it. Just another senseless shooting on the South Side. As if that's all we do, shoot each other." She sounded bitter.

"Do you know what's going to happen? I mean, can she get the boy buried?"

Barbara shrugged. "I'm not sure how much money Deborah has. She's probably broke. You know she's renting

the house she's in. Maybe I should call Lorraine or Donna or the church secretary. Maybe we can raise some money for her if she doesn't have any."

"But she doesn't even go to our church."

Barbara's look made her feel ashamed of her words. "That doesn't mean we can't show her some love. She's gonna need it."

Tears sprang to Lela's eyes as she recalled the Holy Spirit's question from a couple of days ago: *Is there room in your heart for him?*

She actually dreaded returning home from the hospital on Tuesday afternoon after getting the cast. And it wasn't just because of the steady snowfall that crept up on them as Barbara drove away from the doctor's office. It was that house—that empty house waiting for her.

Barbara parked in front and left the car running. "Use the front door, Sid," she suggested as Sidney hoisted Lela out of the car, only bumping her slippered foot once. "That okay, Le?"

That was fine with Lela. She was not up to seeing the garage looming in the backyard—the scene of the murder.

She didn't even blink as Sidney carried her into the house, tracking snow on the carpet.

A bouquet of pink, green, and white balloons sat on the coffee table. And there was also a floral arrangement on the dining room table just beyond the living room.

"Lorraine dropped off the balloons and flowers," Barbara explained, as she waved a cream-mittened hand. "The balloons are from our Bible study and the flowers are from the usher board. Donna put you on the list for meals to be delivered for a couple of weeks till you get on your feet good. There are some already in your freezer, so you won't have to cook for a while. And Pastor said the youth group's gonna send someone to shovel your snow."

"Thank you." Lela wanted to feel grateful for the support and evident love from the women. But she just felt numb. A boy was dead. And she hadn't cared about him when he was alive.

Sidney settled her on the couch, then slapped a leather cap on his head. "I'll be in the car, Moms. Take care, Mrs. Edwards." He quickly headed out the front door.

"You sure you wanna be here?" Barbara asked. "You're not feeling spooked about Ronnie, are you?"

Lela shrugged off her coat. "I'll be all right." Truth to tell, she *was* rattled. And she was grateful for the excuse of having nowhere to go. She could avoid the garage for the time being. "Where's Smokey?"

"Under your bed, probably. Al said he retreated there, whenever he wasn't eating."

Lela nodded. He was probably mad at her for leaving him. She seemed to make everyone mad lately.

Barbara's look was keen as she placed a couch pillow under Lela's foot and another one at her back. "You didn't have to rush off, y'know. You're always welcome to come back home with me and boss me around."

Lela didn't crack a smile. "I called Frank," she said quietly. "My niece Catherine is coming to stay a couple of days until I decide what to do."

The smile promptly disappeared from Barbara's face. "Decide what to do about what?"

"About Christmas, about moving."

Barbara sank onto the other end of the couch. "But I thought you didn't wanna move."

Lela sighed. "Maybe I should."

"Are you worried because of what happened to Ronnie?"

"Barb, I don't know *what* to think."

Barbara stood. "Maybe, instead of making a snap decision, you should pray about it." She headed into the kitchen.

Why didn't I think of that? She hadn't prayed at all today.

Barbara returned to the living room, carrying the red tote bag. "When you don't know what to do, trust that God does." She set the bag down. "Keep your foot elevated. Keep your soul elevated, while you're at it."

Keep your soul elevated?

Ten minutes after Barbara left, Lela heard a soft yowl that increased in volume. Soon there was Smokey, striding into the living room. But instead of giving her the view of his back as he sometimes did when angry, he strolled over and nudged her hand. But he didn't jump into her lap, demanding attention, as he normally would. Instead, in two hops he was perched on top of the couch, as if watching over her.

She tried to pray but didn't quite know what to pray. Questions like *Lord, why this, why now?* came to mind in regard to her ankle, and about Ronnie's death.

Elevate your soul, Barbara said. I need my Bible. Barbara

had placed it and the sheet with the assigned Scriptures from Bible study on top of the pieced quilt blocks. She turned to the sixth passage on the list, Matthew 2—the Magi's visit to Jesus. *Might as well read the seventh one as well, since it's in the same chapter.*

MATTHEW 2:1–15

Now when Jesus was born in Bethlehem of Judea in the days of Herod the king, behold, there came wise men from the east to Jerusalem, saying, Where is he that is born King of the Jews? for we have seen his star in the east, and are come to worship him. When Herod the king had heard these things, he was troubled, and all Jerusalem with him. And when he had gathered all the chief priests and scribes of the people together, he demanded of them where Christ should be born. And they said unto him, In Bethlehem of Judea: for thus it is written by the prophet, And thou Bethlehem, in the land of Juda, art not the least among the princes of Juda: for out of thee shall come a Governor, that shall rule my people Israel. Then Herod, when he had privily called the wise men, inquired of them diligently what time the star appeared. And he sent them

to Bethlehem, and said, Go and search diligently for the young child; and when ye have found him, bring me word again, that I may come and worship him also. When they had heard the king, they departed; and, lo, the star, which they saw in the east, went before them, till it came and stood over where the young child was. When they saw the star, they rejoiced with exceeding great joy. And when they were come into the house, they saw the young child with Mary his mother, and fell down, and worshipped him: and when they had opened their treasures, they presented unto him gifts; gold, and frankincense and myrrh. And being warned of God in a dream that they should not return to Herod, they departed into their own country another way. And when they were departed, behold, the angel of the Lord appeareth to Joseph in a dream, saying, Arise, and take the young child and his mother, and flee into Egypt, and be thou there until I bring thee word: for Herod will seek the young child to destroy him. When he arose, he took the young child and his mother by night, and departed into Egypt: and was there until the death of Herod: that it might be fulfilled which was spoken of the Lord by the prophet, saying, Out of Egypt have I called my son.

Afterward, she quickly pulled the pattern out of the bag and stared in awe at the toy chest for the sixth block and the toy car for the seventh. She laughed a breathless laugh. The toy chest could be made into a treasure chest to fit the gifts of the Magi. The quilt was starting to look more and more like a tribute to Mary's life.

She settled back on the couch, savoring Matthew 2 once again. What was life like for Mary and Joseph before the Magi came, bearing their expensive gifts? Were they barely able to make ends meet? Did they worry about how they would survive? What truths did they hold on to, even without knowing how God would work out the situation?

The gifts brought by the Magi were fit for a king. Did these gifts allow them to finally breathe easier?

She couldn't help recalling the year Tamara was born, 1961. She hadn't quite finished the certification process. The burden was on Walter to provide for their family.

It seemed that in those days they argued most often over money. There weren't any Magi bearing expensive gifts on camels. They'd had to ask Walter's parents for money—

money Walter's parents barely had themselves. But God had provided, just as he provided for Mary and Joseph.

Lela picked up the pattern once more. The car seemed to fit the rest of the story as Mary, Joseph, and Jesus escaped to Egypt.

How desperate Mary and Joseph must have felt, waking up in the middle of the night and having to "get out of Dodge." What choice did they have, with Herod out for Jesus' blood? Did Mary worry about hiding Jesus? It was hard to imagine hiding God's Son anyway. There he was—the riches of heaven—on the run for his life. Mary had to trust that God would protect her family.

So why didn't he protect Ronnie? The thought came unbidden and caused her mood to plummet once again. She knew she needed to pray. *Lord, did you allow this to happen to force me to move? You told Mary and Joseph when to move and when to return home. Is this my time to move?*

y four that afternoon, there was still no sign of Catherine but even more snow.

Eileen called, asking, "Did you know that at least four people stopped at your garage today? Just checking out the scene of the murder, I guess."

Lela wondered how she knew the exact number. Was she peeping out her window the whole time?

"One lady even had a cell phone out taking pictures. I marched right out to that garage to send her on her way."

Lela could have done without that information. Before she could make an excuse to get off the phone, Eileen added, "If you wouldn't mind praying for Daddy, I'd appreciate it. He's not feeling too well today. I had to take a sick day just to look after him."

"I'll try to remember to do so. Do you need anything?"

Not that she could do much of anything. But she could call the church and have Eileen and her father put on the prayer list.

She thought Deborah could use a prayer or at least some encouragement too. But what do you say to a woman whose child has just been shot, she wondered—a child who will never see fourteen, never make it to a high school dance?

After an argument with herself, she dialed Deborah's number.

All hope of simply leaving a message was dashed when Deborah answered the phone. "Hello?" There was a pitiable hollow edge to Deborah's voice.

"This is Lela Edwards from across the street."

"Oh. Hi."

Lela almost lost courage at the bleakness of Deborah's response. "I'm sorry about your boy."

The subsequent silence felt awkward. Just as Lela tried to work out what to say to bridge the gap, Deborah blurted out, "For what it's worth, he didn't break in to your garage. I know he didn't. He doesn't do things like that. . . . Usually, he doesn't. But . . . I found a bag under his bed. It has your credit card receipt in it."

So he *did* steal Darcie's present. Lela felt a horrible sense of disappointment. She hadn't realized until now that she'd held on to a slight hope that maybe he *hadn't* stolen it.

Deborah's voice broke. "Ronnie tried to borrow money from my ex-husband. My ex just told me a few minutes ago. That's why it's funny that you called now. . . . But he didn't have the money, y'know? He got laid off last month and was trying to find another job."

"Money for what?"

"I think Ronnie wanted to give me a present for Christmas. So, he . . . stole your bag. . . . I couldn't show it to the police. I just couldn't. . . . Not after . . ."

Lela sighed, torn between pity and horror. "Keep it."

"I'm really sorry. He shouldn't have—"

"Just keep it, okay? I don't . . . want it back." She fumbled for the button to hang up the phone. Instead of putting it on the coffee table, she held on to the slim, blue phone as if it were a lifeline—a link to a life that was forever altered now by one boy's death.

She didn't know how long she sat there with the phone in her hand and shadows gathering in the living room—the usual business of dusk. But as the Christmas lights flickered

on across the street, she suddenly realized that Catherine was still not there. She quickly dialed Frank's number.

Rhoda answered the phone on the fifth ring. "Cee Cee tried to call you, but your line was busy. She's on her way, but with the snow, it's slow going. And she got a bit of a late start."

Since the curtains were still open, Lela could see the snow blowing by as if in a hurry for an appointment. After a pause she said, "Tell the girl to turn back. . . . I can manage."

"You sure? I'd hate for you to be by yourself there with a broken ankle. Surely you need help around the—"

"I'll manage." She hung up, seared by a disappointment she didn't have long to ponder over, as the phone rang almost immediately.

"Did your niece get there?" asked Barbara over the hum of laughter in the background.

"Not coming."

"Why don't you call Deborah? Let me give you her number."

"Have you lost your mind? I can't impose on her at a time like—"

Is there room in your heart? Once again she could hear

the soft voice of the Holy Spirit. Was he asking her about Deborah—to accept her, to welcome her? How would asking her to come over and clean be welcoming? She paused, before saying, "I already *have* her number, thank you. Anyway, I don't see—"

"*She* needs to get out of that house. *You* need somebody with you. Quit being so stubborn and admit that you need somebody!"

"If I'm supposed to call her, why are you still talking to me?"

"Get off the phone then, girl!" She could hear Barbara chuckling as she clicked the button on her cell phone to end the conversation.

Deborah's line went to voicemail. She debated about leaving a message and wound up leaving a quick "Barbara told me to call you," before hanging up.

About forty-five minutes passed before the doorbell rang, but after a few seconds, a figure in a red wool coat and a scarf came in, stamping snow on her carpet.

"It's just me," said Deborah. "I got your message. Barbara called also and told me you needed help. She said to just walk in. Was that okay?"

Lela grunted an assent. "Closet's over there." She nodded to the closet opposite the front door.

"I'm glad you called earlier." Deborah hung up her coat, snow still sliding off of it. "Thank you." She perched on the edge of the chair by the door, her hands tightly folded.

There was silence, one that threatened to last for a while. Lela knew that she needed to be the one to break it, to give in. "How you holding up?"

"My supervisor gave me some days off. So I have a lot of free time." Her voice sounded as if tears were shortly to come. "I like to keep busy. . . . Afternoons and nights are hard, though." She paused to sigh.

"Where you from originally? Were you born and raised in Chicago?"

"I lived with my grandmama till I was eight. We used to live on Forty-seventh Street. She passed when I was eight."

"What about your parents?"

"My daddy died when I was three. Car accident. My grandmama used to say Mama didn't know anything about raising kids. Me and Mama got an apartment on Seventy-eighth. She's still over there."

Lela didn't want to ask this but felt compelled to say, "How old were you when Ronnie was born?"

"Sixteen. Got married at eighteen to Ronnie's daddy, finally. We were too young. We stayed together until Ronnie was seven, though. I probably shouldn't have divorced him." She smiled. "Ronnie was just like his daddy. Real smart, y'know? Said he wanted to be a teacher."

Lela flinched at the mention of her profession. *Do tell.*

"He was always showing the younger kids how to do things. He told me that the teacher he had this year inspired him."

"I wish . . ." Lela forced herself to go on, pricked by the pain of a lost opportunity. "I wish I'd known him."

Deborah sighed heavily. "I thought I was protecting him by moving him out this way. Keeping him out the gangs in the old 'hood. And now . . . now he'll never know . . . this baby." She patted her rounded stomach. "She'll be born this spring. . . . I wish he could be here to see her. Y'know what's silly? I still find myself looking at the clock around three twenty-six every afternoon. That's when Ronnie used to come home from . . ." Her voice ended, not in a sob, but

with her slowly beating her fists against her thighs, her body shaking with a grief that caused the tears to spring to Lela's eyes.

Here she was feeling sorry for herself and also thinking herself superior to Deborah. But there Deborah was just days after her son's murder sitting in her living room offering her help. She hadn't wanted to be around the girl, hadn't wanted to see her grief—a grief she could no longer ignore.

Lord Jesus, help me make it up to this girl. Not knowing what else to do, she struggled up on the crutches and moved to awkwardly place her right hand on Deborah's head.

"It's gonna be all right," she whispered, not sure if it was, but determined to play a part in the righting of it, nevertheless.

Deborah wiped her eyes with her sleeve. Lela decided to forgo pointing to the tissue box at her elbow. "Got something for me to do?"

"There's some washing downstairs."

"Okay. Anything else?"

"I can make a list."

She wound up vacuuming, washing dishes, dusting, and feeding Smokey as well. Lela itched to check the dishes to

make sure they were up to her specifications. But she decided to let that go.

By seven, the list was done. "Want me to heat you up something in the microwave?" Deborah asked.

"I can manage. Thank you for coming by." For the first time, she meant it. "'Preciate all you've done."

Deborah slowly retrieved her coat from the closet. "Well, I guess I'd better get back across the street. Take care, Miss Lela."

Miss Lela. Lela nodded at the evidence of good home training. "You too."

As soon as Deborah left, she realized that she could have asked her to stay and eat with her. *Maybe some other time.*

She called Barbara, who answered after six rings. "I almost didn't recognize your number. You're on your cell phone."

"Just called to say stay outta my business, old nosy woman!"

"Now what did I do?"

Lela merely laughed.

Barbara chuckled. "I take it Deborah was a help. I knew she would be. Feeling better?"

Lela grunted. Actually, she was. *Thank you, Jesus.*

14

ama," said Jean, when she called on Wednesday, "I've been thinking and praying, and Chris and I talked about this . . ." The pause after her words seemed to go on for a long time. Never had Jean seemed so hesitant to speak. "Since you seem so resistant, Chris thinks maybe I was wrong to push you into moving here."

Lela put her sewing down, even though she'd turned on the speaker on her cell phone. "So now you don't *want* me to move near you?"

"Mama, you don't have to make what I said into a negative."

"I'm just trying to understand you."

"Are you really?"

Lela opened and closed her mouth. Maybe she wasn't really.

"I was thinking that maybe . . . maybe God wants you there for now."

Maybe God wants you there. Jean's words ran through her mind even after the conversation ended. She hadn't particularly wanted to move, even though the neighborhood had declined over the years. And she *was* getting older. Perhaps she wouldn't always be able to take care of herself. Maybe someday she'd have to make that decision to move closer to family. But maybe, just maybe, someday wasn't today.

She gazed at the bird she'd cut out for the eighth block, then at the other seven blocks of the quilt top. There was no question about it. This was more than just a baby quilt. It was a memory quilt, with a small snapshot of Mary's journey stitched into each square. Like this bird.

Before Jean called, she'd listened to the story in Leviticus 12:1–8 of Jesus' presentation in the temple and Mary and Joseph offering two birds as a sacrifice.

Look at God, she marveled. *He's done this.* Perhaps

that was all God required of her—to make a sacrifice of his choosing. And he seemed to choose her to give up her will, her plan. He'd wanted her to make the quilt.

LEVITICUS 12:1–8

And the LORD spake unto Moses, saying, Speak unto the children of Israel, saying, If a woman have conceived seed, and borne a man child: then she shall be unclean seven days; according to the days of the separation for her infirmity shall she be unclean. And in the eighth day the flesh of his foreskin shall be circumcised. And she shall then continue in the blood of her purifying three and thirty days; she shall touch no hallowed thing, nor come into the sanctuary, until the days of her purifying be fulfilled. But if she bear a maid child, then she shall be unclean two weeks, as in her separation: and she shall continue in the blood of her purifying threescore and six days. And when the days of her purifying are fulfilled, for a son, or for a daughter, she shall bring a lamb of the first year for a burnt offering, and a young pigeon, or a turtledove, for a sin offering, unto the door of the tabernacle of the congregation, unto the priest: who shall offer it before the

LORD, and make an atonement for her; and she shall be cleansed from the issue of her blood. This is the law for her that hath borne a male or a female. And if she be not able to bring a lamb, then she shall bring two turtles, or two young pigeons; the one for the burnt offering, and the other for a sin offering: and the priest shall make an atonement for her, and she shall be clean.

"Mama, I think you should consider moving." Tamara's voice was firm when she called that afternoon. "Maybe Jean's right. Maybe you *should* move to Missouri City or Houston as she suggested."

But not Reston, Virginia? She couldn't help noticing that Tamara *hadn't* suggested that she move closer to *her* family.

Lela leaned against the arm of the couch, watching a group of what she assumed to be teens loitering on the sidewalk in front of her house. People did that more and more, now that a murder had taken place in the alley behind her house.

"The neighborhood's not all it used to be. That could have been *you*, y'know, or some other innocent bystander."

"But it *wasn't* me."

"Mama—"

"I've got some good news though. Got a letter from the Social Security office. They finally decided that I'm alive." Lela chuckled, but Tamara didn't.

"Mama, that could have been you. If you hadn't gone to the hospital . . ."

But she had. If she hadn't fallen down the stairs, she would have been home when it happened. Was that God's way of protecting her or at least removing her from the situation? After all, she hadn't broken a hip. And her ankle wasn't as badly broken as it could have been. All in all, he had been merciful. She felt almost weak with a mixture of gratitude and horror at what had happened.

Suddenly, she didn't feel like talking about it anymore. "Thank you for the Christmas gift, by the way."

"Knowing you, it's already spent."

"Um, sort of. I'm thinking about taking back the shoes I got and getting something cheaper, like a wallet."

"A wallet? Whatever for?"

"I want to donate the rest of the money to the benevolence fund at church. Thank you all the same, Tam."

But Tamara was laughing. "Well, it's your gift to do what you want. Just thought you wanted some nice shoes."

"Some people don't have jobs, Tam."

"Is this a lecture, Mama?" Tamara sounded irritated.

Lela bristled but suddenly laughed instead. "I guess I *do* lecture, don't I? You know how your mama is. Anyway, I need to get off this phone. Got some quilting to do. I need my hands free."

"You could have used the speaker phone."

"Give Stan my love."

"Will do."

She pulled her red tote bag closer and began piecing together the last block—a cheerful-looking brown teddy bear on a peacock blue background. Oh, did that bring back memories, mostly of Jean carrying around a ratty brown teddy bear, one that had been given to her at Christmas. Separating her from that bear was almost impossible. Oh, how Jean pitched a fit when Lela'd finally thrown the filthy thing out. At the time it seemed the right thing to do for a nine-year-old. Now she wasn't so sure.

Walt had sided with the child. "You're too hard on Jeannie sometimes, Le," he'd said. "She's not you. Take her for what she is."

She'd scoffed then. What she was, was often moody and

complaining. She was Walt's favorite, although he often denied it.

"I love all my children equally," he claimed. Yet he spent the most time with Jean, watching TV with her, teaching her to draw. Both claimed to love science fiction, which Lela didn't care one way or the other about.

Jean loved hanging with her daddy. Now that she thought about it, she'd always felt a little jealous of their close relationship. Walt always seemed to take the time to listen to Jean's constant chatter, which wore her out. But Walt never seemed to feel that way. He seemed to understand her, to delight in the way that she explored the world with such fierce curiosity.

Did Mary feel as she felt with Jean, as she listened to her son in the temple firing questions at the temple leaders? She turned to the last Scripture on the Bible study sheet—Luke 2, beginning at verse 43—and read the account of Jesus' being found in the temple.

LUKE 2:43–51

And when they had fulfilled the days, as they returned, the child Jesus tarried behind in Jerusalem; and Joseph

and his mother knew not of it. But they, supposing him to have been in the company, went a day's journey; and they sought him among their kinsfolk and acquaintance. And when they found him not, they turned back again to Jerusalem, seeking him. And it came to pass, that after three days they found him in the temple, sitting in the midst of the doctors, both hearing them, and asking them questions. And all that heard him were astonished at his understanding and answers. And when they saw him, they were amazed: and his mother said unto him, Son, why hast thou thus dealt with us? behold, thy father and I have sought thee sorrowing. And he said unto them, How is it that ye sought me? wist ye not that I must be about my Father's business? And they understood not the saying which he spake unto them. And he went down with them, and came to Nazareth, and was subject unto them: but his mother kept all these sayings in her heart.

Did Mary look at him as if she didn't understand what would make him say the things that He said? Did she see him as both wonderfully brilliant and exasperating, even though he was the Son of God?

She sat back, remembering Deborah's frantic search for Ronnie. Did she see him the same way—as brilliant but exasperating, someone she couldn't help fiercely loving and wanting to fiercely protect?

She was still pondering the matter when Barbara called forty minutes later. "The block club's collecting money to buy a nice arrangement for Ronnie's funeral," said Barbara. "Think you can contribute anything to the wake? I'm keeping the list."

Lela sighed. "You know I'm not doing much cooking these—"

"It'll be after Christmas, because of the postmortem. Also, the funeral home is kind of backed up, because of the holidays. By the way, the funeral will probably be held at A. R. Leak on Seventy-eighth and Cottage."

"Way over there?"

"Deb's got relatives over there. They're helping her with the funeral expenses."

"Is she moving back over there near them?"

"I don't think they invited her. But she might not have a choice."

"What do you mean?"

"She moved into the house because her boyfriend was helping pay the rent. But now that he's gone, I don't see how she can afford it. You know the Davises were renting their house to her. They can't cut her a break for long, even being friends of her auntie."

"Surprised she's not on welfare."

"She's *trying* to stay off of it, Le."

Lela sighed again, this time over her assumptions about Deborah. Instead of giving money to the church's benevolence fund, maybe she should give it to Deborah. "I guess Christmas will be hard for her. Does she have somewhere to go? She probably needs to get out of that house."

"Speaking of getting out of that house, did you look at your garage yet? You know the police want to know if anything's been taken. You're the only one who can tell that."

"And how do you expect me to get out to the garage with a broken ankle?"

"Crutches. And if I'm not mistaken, somebody's coming by today to make sure the snow's shoveled. Whoever it is can help make sure you don't fall and break the other one."

Barbara had been right as usual, although Lela wouldn't tell her that. The tall, very thin young man from the youth group (Estelle's boy, looked like his mama spit him out) acted as her spotter as she slowly made her way down the freshly shoveled walkway to the garage. At least his pants didn't look as if they would slide off any second like those of many of the young men around the neighborhood. He didn't grab her arm as she feared he would. Instead he walked beside her, his hand out slightly as if ready to grab her if she started to fall.

She noted with approval the salt he'd sprinkled on the ground and hoped he'd done the same in the front.

"You good, Mrs. Edwards?" He looked as if he wanted to get back to his task.

At her nod, he returned to shoveling the slab on the side of the garage while she stood in front of the open door, feeling a mixture of emotions. The Camry was intact. Walt's tools remained in the tool chest at the back of the garage. There was nothing missing that she could tell. The lawn mower still sat in its usual place against the wall on the right.

"It was bound to happen."

She nearly jumped out of her skin at the sound of James's voice. There he was in the alley, leaning against his cane. It was

35 degrees or so, and he wore a long-sleeved, tan flannel shirt and gray pants. No coat to speak of. One suspender hung off his shoulder. "You nearly scared me to death! What are you doing out here in the cold without a coat? Thought you were sick in bed."

"It was bound to happen," he said again. "Boys like that get killed every day."

"Well, he might have made something of himself." Her own words surprised her. *He might have, at that. Instead he lived a short, sad life.*

"Sometimes you have to take the law into your own hands." James's hands seemed to shake as he lifted his, as if pleading for something.

"What's that?"

"The law. Sometimes you have to." His voice was quiet, not like his usual bombast. It almost sounded as if he were trying to convince himself that what he said was true.

His eyes didn't look right. She wondered if he had a fever. "You better get inside. It's cold out."

She soon heard the slam of a window being thrown open. "Daddy!" Eileen called. "Daddy! Where are you?"

"Coming. I'm coming."

"Daddy!"

"I said I'm coming!"

Lela shook her head as she watched him shuffle through the slush. "Sometimes you have to take the law into your own hands," he'd said. But as the meaning of his words slowly dawned on her, she gazed at his back in horror. Could he have followed his own advice?

Lord, Lord, what am I gonna do?

In the end, what needed to be done seemed about to be done for her.

"Eileen called. James is in the hospital," Barbara said on Thursday, Christmas Eve. "Had a massive stroke last night. Eileen thinks he's not likely to make it."

"Maybe he shouldn't," Lela said quietly.

"Lela!"

"I think he killed that boy, Barb. Something he said the other day about taking the law into our hands."

Now it was Barbara's turn to be silent. "You're jumping to conclusions."

"Barbara, he came out and talked to me while I was looking at the garage. I saw his face. I think he killed that boy."

Barbara didn't say anything for several moments. "He

was convinced that Ronnie had broken into their garage and yours."

"Do you know if he had a gun? You seem to know everything else."

Barbara shrugged. "Probably did. What a mess."

"I *told* Eileen she couldn't handle having him live with her."

"We don't know for sure that he killed Ronnie. It could've been Leo or his new girlfriend. The Volkswagen was registered to her."

"Anybody she knows could've driven that car." When she didn't hear an immediate response to her statement, Lela added, "Hello? Hello?"

"I'm here. I'm just . . . surprised, that's all. Surprised you'd say that. Thought you'd have a definite opinion is all."

Lela started to utter a retort but kept silent. Maybe she *had* been venting her opinions a bit too freely.

"Are you gonna tell the police?" Barbara asked.

"I have to, don't you think? At least, I have to tell them what James said. Whether or not that adds up to his having killed Ronnie, well, that's up to them. . . . This is gonna break Eileen's heart."

"I don't think he'll live long enough to stand trial if the police arrest him."

"He still has to answer for what he did, if he did it."

Before the end of that day, he might be answering directly to the Lord, if what Barbara guessed came to pass, Lela mused. Maybe that was God's way of justice. It was a far more merciful end than what was given to Ronnie. Her eyes filled with tears. She put down the phone and wept for Ronnie.

She wept, remembering the times she had complained about the possibility of someone like Ronnie breaking into her garage. Had James in his own twisted way taken her complaints as a license for him to murder that boy?

Did Mary weep when she heard about the children who were murdered because of her son? Did she wail at God like their mamas probably did, wondering why He didn't help those innocent children?

Why God? Why didn't you help that boy?

And in her heart, she heard a whisper, *Lela, why didn't you?*

"So, sis, have you changed your mind about coming out tomorrow?" Frank asked, when he called later that evening.

"Christmas won't be the same without you. . . . Rhoda'll pick you up."

Lela set down the quilt, even though she'd already turned on the speaker phone. "I'll come, but only if I can bring a guest."

"Who? Don't tell me you're dating now."

"Have you lost your mind? No, I meant my neighbor."

"The old man next door?"

"Boy, don't play with me." She didn't want to talk about James. Not now.

Frank laughed. "Barbara? She's always welcome here."

"No. I mean the one whose son was killed."

Frank was silent for a beat as if digesting the news. "I heard about that. Maybe you should think about moving, sis."

"Don't you start again. Why is everyone trying to get me to move?"

"The 'hood's not what it used to be when you first moved out there. That's why I'm out this way."

"You're out that way because your kids and grandkids keep trying to move back home and you needed a bigger house."

Frank chuckled. "I know that's right. Anyway, come on through. Bring anybody you want. Bud and Angela are coming and they're bringing fried turkey."

"I hope he replaced the last turkey fryer that nearly burned down his garage."

"Uh, I'm not sure. It'll be a great Christmas."

Lela suddenly felt a vein of joy she hadn't imagined she would ever feel after hearing what James had to say. Inviting Deborah to Frank's felt right. "I could sure use one."

She gazed at the quilt top she was now starting to sew together. A quilt wouldn't bring Deborah's boy back, or bring his murderer to justice. But a quilt was a promise—a promise that God would watch out for her and the baby. She didn't have much else to give, did she?

Is there room in your heart? That was a question God had asked more than once.

Lela got up with a grunt and made her way down the hall. She was getting much better at using the crutches. And right now, she wanted to look at the girls' room—the one Jean and Sylvie used to have. The space was empty. But maybe it didn't have to be. After all, there was room, if Deborah needed it—room for two more.

"Hey, Grannie Le."

Only Darcie called her that. "Darcie. So good to hear your voice, dear. Hold on just a second. I want to switch to the speaker." She switched it on before picking up her quilt, shooing Smokey away from it. He was her shadow these days, always following her and having to be near her.

"You must be working on something."

"A baby quilt. I'm almost done with the top. Then I'll start making the sandwich."

"Did you say a *baby* quilt? I thought you *never* made those."

"There's a first time for everything."

"That's so sweet of you. I was wondering when I was finally going to get one of your quilts."

"Maybe I'll make you one after this. But this isn't for you."

Darcie chuckled. "That's cold, Grannie."

"No offense. It's for a neighbor who just lost her son. She's coming to stay here for a while—just till she gets on her feet."

"Oh. I heard about that."

"From who?"

"Uncle Frank. You know he blabs everything. He said you talked about it on Christmas. Listen, Grannie . . ." Her voice trailed off. Lela had the feeling she was trying to find the words to make up for Christmas. It was hard to believe that Christmas had come and gone already. Here it was December 28 already.

"It's okay, Darcie. Everything worked out for the best this Christmas. It was different than I thought it would be, but I enjoyed myself at Frank's, aside from the broken ankle." She waited a few beats before adding, "I'm sorry about Doug."

"Are you mad?"

"Why would I be mad at you?"

"I know how you feel about divorce. And I didn't come out to see you this Christmas."

"Honey, I understand." And she did. She understood wanting to hide away from the world, wanting to hide from those you were afraid would judge you.

"I never told anybody this, but when your granddaddy and I had been married about thirteen years, we had some serious problems. We talked about separating."

"Mama never told me that. Well, she told me you and Granddaddy were fighting a lot one time, which scared her. She didn't understand what was going on. You think that helped her want to be a marriage and family therapist?"

Lela started to ask how a nine-year-old even knew that therapy was a career path, but instead she said, "Maybe." Anything was possible. And maybe, just maybe, God had that career path in mind for her all along.

"Mama wants to talk to you."

Jean came on the phone. "Mother, when are you coming out to visit? Notice I said 'visit.' I'm not gonna nag you about moving anymore."

"I'll come in January. And I'll keep thinking about it, honey. Moving that is. For now, I'll stay. I'm needed here."

Jean sighed. "Okay, Mother. You're right. Just . . . know that I need you too."

Lela smiled. She'd raised her daughters to be independent. But it sure was nice to be needed sometimes.

"You wanna hold her?"

"Of course."

Deborah smiled as she lifted the sleeping infant out of the crib. "Careful now."

"Girl, I have held my share of babies, thank you."

Deborah nodded. "I'm sorry! I'm sorry! You're right."

Nevertheless, Lela accepted the sleeping newborn with a carefulness she hadn't displayed in a long time. She marveled at the tiny fingers, the closed eyelids, the wispy black hair, and the general baby smell of her. She couldn't trace any likeness of Leo. This baby was all her mama's, even down to the heart-shaped face, pert nose, and bronze skin.

She turned her attention away from the baby to look with satisfaction over the room. Three months had brought a few changes. The crib sat in the corner underneath the window, where Jean's twin bed used to go. The other twin bed, Sylvie's, still occupied the space nearest the closet. The room was just the place for a new baby—a spring baby— even though the blue of the walls was the same blue from thirty years ago.

Even Smokey seemed to find the arrangements to his satisfaction, judging by the fact that he was currently curled up on the baby's diaper bag.

"Hold her for a second. I have something I want to give her."

Lela returned the baby to her mother's outstretched arms, before reaching into the plastic bag she'd placed on the dresser and pulling out the memory quilt. "Now that she's finally home, I can give this to you."

She handed Deborah the quilt, remembering how God's grace had come in so many unexpected ways at Christmas. It was like the white fabric she'd chosen for the background—something that united all the events of that season.

"That's the quilt you were making at Christmas, right? It's beautiful! You can see it when you wake up, Lela."

Lela smiled. To think the child named the baby after her . . .

"Can I?" Deborah added, as she began wrapping the quilt around the baby.

"Here, let me." Lela soon got the quilt and the baby situated in her arms. "Little girl," she whispered, "when you wake up, I wanna tell you a story about a lady who only wanted what was best for her kids." She patted the quilt—her handiwork. Pretty good, if she had to say so herself. "This memory quilt reminds me of her story."

"You're talking about Mary, right? I know you said you were reading about her at Christmas."

"True that, true that. But right now"—she looked up at Deborah and smiled—"I'm talking about you."

ACKNOWLEDGMENTS

*C*hristmas is a time for family and reflection on the favor of God. This holiday season, I pray that you are surrounded with the radiating glow of love from your family and friends.

I would like to thank my family at Atria Books for their continued support. Thank you to Judith Curr, Carolyn Reidy, and Christine Saunders, for understanding the importance of this project and helping to bring it to life. A special note to Malaika Adero for her editorial prowess and anointed gift of patience. I am also grateful to Ayo Morris and the TDJE team for their tireless efforts and commitment to my creative endeavors.

My deep and overwhelming gratitude to Jan Miller and Shannon Marven at Dupree Miller & Associates. Thank you for your passion for and commitment to excellence.

LIFE

A Favored Person:

1. endures, even though she may be the center of gossip.

2. doesn't need a man to fulfill God's plan.

3. ponders things deeply before spouting an opinion.

4. experiences God's mercy.

5. praises no matter what the circumstances.

LESSONS

6. is still favored, even when a divorce is pending.

7. is still obedient, even when he doesn't fully understand the situation.

8. sometimes faces inhospitable people, pain, and loss.

9. makes room for the Savior and anyone else God sends.

10. sees the culmination of God's promises.